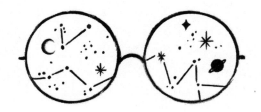

EX LIBRIS:

....

Clara Voyant

Clara Voyant

RACHELLE DELANEY

PUFFIN

an imprint of Penguin Random House Canada Young Readers,
a Penguin Random House Company

First published 2018

1 2 3 4 5 6 7 8 9 10 (LSC)

Manufactured in the U.S.A.

Library and Archives Canada Cataloguing in Publication
Delaney, Rachelle, author
     Clara Voyant / Rachelle Delaney.

Issued in print and electronic formats.
ISBN 978-0-14-319853-6 (hardcover). —ISBN 978-0-14-319855-0 (EPUB)

     I. Title.
PS8607.E48254C58 2018   jC813'.6   C2017-904335-8
                                             C2017-904336-6

Library of Congress Control Number: 2017945563

Book design by Jennifer Griffiths

www.penguinrandomhouse.ca

Penguin
Random House
PUFFIN CANADA

FOR TARYN

CLARA COSTA HAD ONLY BEEN AT Kensington Middle School for a month, but already she understood the implications of a Blazer Day. All the Newsies did. When Wesley Ferris, editor-in-chief of the Kensington Middle School *Gazette*, showed up to school wearing a blazer, she meant business.

So when the last bell rang on Tuesday afternoon, Clara was ready. She'd been watching the clock tick steadily toward 3:15 all through math class. The second it hit, she slammed her textbook shut, hopped out of her desk, and beelined for her meeting.

Unfortunately, it was hard to get anywhere fast at Kensington Middle School, or KMS as the students called it. KMS was enormous—easily three times the size of High Park Public, where Clara had gone to elementary school—and jam-packed with what felt like three hundred times as many kids (though it was probably closer to ten).

They surrounded her in the hallway, sweeping her along with them as they surged toward their lockers, laughing and shouting.

"Excuse me." She tried to push her way across the hall. "Um, can I get through? I've got to—"

A basketball sailed over her head and smacked the wall. Some kids gasped. Others guffawed.

"Watch it," someone warned. *"She's* around here somewhere."

Everyone paused to glance over their shoulders, including Clara. But Mrs. Major, the KMS custodian, was nowhere in sight. Relieved, she continued on, picking up the pace but being careful not to break into a run. Mrs. Major's Number One Rule—even more important than No Throwing Basketballs—was No Running in the Halls. And Mrs. Major was not to be disobeyed. Mrs. Major was even more intimidating than Wesley Ferris in a blazer.

Farther down the hallway, a crowd of kids had gathered outside the auditorium, chattering excitedly. Clara thought she could hear her best friend, Maeve, among the other voices, but she couldn't stop to check; her meeting was starting in roughly three minutes.

She hung a sharp right into the hallway that led to Mr. Banerjee's classroom, nearly colliding with a group of older girls snapping photos of each other with their phones. Or rather, she realized once she was safely out of their way, they were all snapping photos of one girl in particular. She had long, curly black hair and wore a dress that could have doubled as a beach towel.

"Ooh, this is a good one." One of the girl's friends held up her phone.

The girl in the towel-dress glanced at it and frowned. "You cut off my feet. The shoes are the most important part." She gestured to her silver slippers, then commanded, "Take it again."

Clara ducked out of the way so she wouldn't photobomb, then hurried on, diving into Mr. Banerjee's classroom just as the clock hit 3:20.

Right on time.

"Clara." Wesley Ferris nodded at her from the head of the table at the back of the room. "Come sit down. We're just getting started."

Clara did as she was told. Because Blazer Day.

Wesley Ferris didn't own just one blazer—she had an *entire collection* of them, each monogrammed on the chest pocket with her initials.

"Rumor has it she gets them *dry cleaned*," Lina Gagliano murmured as Clara dropped into a chair beside her.

"Sorry?" Clara turned to her.

Lina tilted her head toward Wesley's blazer, and Clara stole another glance at the editor-in-chief. Today, her blazer was a crisp white, unblemished by even the smallest splash of grape juice or speck of ketchup (Clara's T-shirt, on the other hand, had both). Her short blond bob curled neatly around the pearls dangling from her earlobes, a few inches above her shoulder pads. "Really?" Clara whispered.

Lina nodded. She flipped her notebook open to a blank page and began to sketch the blazer. Lina was the *Gazette*'s comic artist.

Clara shook her head in wonder. She wouldn't even know where to *find* a dry cleaner. She doubted even her mother would know. Gaby Costa definitely wasn't the dry cleaning type.

Clara's grandmother Elaine was, though—or she had been when she still lived in Toronto. Elaine was also a big fan of blazers, especially in neutral colors like beige and gray and taupe. Clara could still picture them all lined up in her closet, evenly spaced and perfectly pressed. Had she taken them with her to the seniors' home in West Palm Beach? Clara wondered. She'd have to ask next time they talked.

"All right, Newsies, let's get started," Wesley said, once her twelve staff members had arrived. "We only have fifty-seven minutes, and this is an important meeting. I mean, *every* meeting is important," she added, "but this one especially. Today we're going to look at our very first issue in print."

Wesley leaned over, picked up a briefcase (an actual *briefcase*! Lina abandoned the blazer and began sketching it instead) and pulled out a stack of newspapers.

"Oooh," the Newsies breathed.

"Hot off the presses!" Wesley set them down on the table. Lina reached for a copy, but Wesley batted her hand away. "Not so fast!"

"Ow!" Lina recoiled.

"There are a few things you need to know first." Wesley held up a finger. "One: the October issue hits newsstands on Friday morning, so everything you see today is top secret until then. Got it? You can't even tell your best friend."

The Newsies nodded.

"Two," Wesley went on, straightening the lapels on her crisp white blazer, "I want you to know how this whole process works, especially you Newbie Newsies." She cast pointed looks at Clara and the few other sixth grade reporters around the table, who'd only joined the *Gazette* three weeks before, shortly after the school year began. "After everyone sent me their articles last week, I got down to work. I spent two days editing tirelessly. Some of the articles *really* needed it."

Clara swallowed, hoping hers wasn't one of them. She planned to send her very first article to Elaine in West Palm Beach, since Elaine was a big fan of what Wesley called "hard-hitting investigative news." Not that Clara's profile of the KMS knitting club was exactly hard-hitting or investigative. But it was an article in print nonetheless.

"Once I finally finished editing, I sent the articles to—" Wesley stopped as the classroom door opened and in walked Mr. Banerjee.

"Oh . . . hi, kids." He blinked at them, as if he hadn't expected to find them in his classroom, although they met there twice a week (after school on Tuesdays and on Fridays at noon).

"Hi, Mr. B.," the Newsies chorused—except for Wesley, who frowned at the interruption.

As one of the English teachers at KMS, Mr. B. had always been in charge of supervising the *Gazette* meetings. But this year, he'd handed over complete control to Wesley. According to Lina Gagliano, who was in seventh grade and seemed to know everything about KMS, there were two reasons for this. First, Mr. B. was retiring at the end of the year and had stopped caring about his *Gazette* duties. And second, Wesley had insisted she needed the leadership experience for her high school portfolio. According to Lina, Wesley planned to attend an arts-focused high school with a renowned journalism program the following year. "So she can really get serious about her career as a newspaper editor," Lina had told Clara, with a roll of her eyes.

Clara had shivered at the thought. She couldn't imagine Wesley getting even *more* serious.

Mr. B. shuffled off to his desk and sat down beside the calendar on which he was counting down the days until his retirement. Today, it read "174."

"As I was saying," Wesley went on, "once I finally finished editing all the articles, I sent them to the production team for layout." She nodded at some kids at the far end of the table. "And when we were satisfied with how it looked, I sent the files to the printer." She started handing out the newspapers. There weren't enough copies for everyone, so Clara shared with Lina.

"The front-page feature looks great," said Lizzie Park, a seventh grade reporter. The Newsies agreed, and Clara did too, though her stomach pinched a little at the sight of it. She'd desperately wanted the feature assignment, which involved investigating whether the tuna in the cafeteria casserole was actually tuna—everyone at KMS had long suspected it wasn't even fish. But Wesley had given it to Ravi Kang, an eighth grade reporter who she said had already "proven his chops." This, Clara had learned, was newspaper-speak for proving you could handle a difficult assignment.

And Ravi *had* done a good job. He'd smuggled a sample of the casserole to the best fishmonger in Kensington Market, who'd declared it not tuna, but canned haddock, cleverly disguised under layers of mayo and soggy croutons. Now the front-page headline demanded, "Will Justice Be Served?" and the article requested the cafeteria staff either start using real tuna or change the casserole's name.

"Real hard-hitting investigative journalism." Wesley nodded. "That's what my—I mean, *our*—newspaper is all about. Keep that in mind, Newsies: I want to see more articles like this."

Clara sighed quietly. She knew she could write a hard-hitting investigative piece—if only Wesley would give her some material to work with.

They flipped to the second page, to the "School Snaps" column by Preston Paisley, a seventh grade photographer. Across the table, Preston straightened and began to polish his camera, which, according to Lina, his parents had bought him over the summer. Clara didn't know much about cameras, but she was pretty certain this one cost more than everything she and her mother owned put together.

At the first *Gazette* meeting of the year, Preston had asked Wesley if he could profile KMS kids who did cool things. "I plan to photograph celebrities when I grow up," he'd explained, lifting his camera and snapping a few photos of the Newsies around the table. Then he'd looked at the images, grimaced and shrugged. "You gotta start somewhere."

"Who's that?" a reporter named Matt pointed to a photo of a girl wearing a coat that looked like a windblown sheepdog. It was, Clara realized, the girl she'd seen in the hallway on her way to the meeting—the one with the beach-towel dress.

"*Who's that?*" Preston blinked at Matt. "What do you mean, *who's that?* It's Olivia Silva!"

Matt shrugged and shook his head. Clara had no idea who she was either, but she wouldn't have admitted it aloud.

"She's probably the most famous kid in school," said Preston. "Definitely the most famous kid in eighth grade."

"She has her own YouTube series, called *KMS Fashionista*," Lina added. "She makes videos about middle-school fashion and makeup trends. It has a pretty big following."

"A *huge* following," Preston added, holding his camera up to his eye. "And she's a great model too. It's tough to find good models around here."

Clara looked down at Preston's photos. They weren't bad, but there was nothing investigative about them. Had it been her assignment, she would have investigated who had made Olivia Silva the authority on middle-school fashion. Also, had any sheepdogs been harmed in the making of her coat?

She kept these questions to herself.

After Preston's column came Lizzie Park's article about the upcoming auditions for the school play. Then came the sports section, with stories from the latest KMS Hornets basketball and soccer games.

Clara was just starting to wonder whether Wesley had forgotten to include her own article when she spotted it, sandwiched between a list of cafeteria lunch specials and the classified ads, at the very back of the paper.

Her stomach sank at the sight.

Why on earth Wesley had insisted Clara profile the school knitting club when there were so many interesting stories at KMS was a mystery. There was little to say about kids who knit socks on their lunch break, and *definitely* nothing investigative.

But Clara had persisted, because as Wesley always said, "Newbie Newsies can't be choosy." And after spending three excruciating lunch hours with the knitters, she'd uncovered what she thought was a decent story: it turned out that according to real scientific studies, some kids listened and concentrated better while they were knitting. So the club was petitioning teachers to let students knit during class.

"Knitwits Fight for Your Right to Stitch!" Clara's headline had declared. It even contained a clever pun. She'd hoped Wesley would be pleased.

But no such luck. Not only had Wesley hidden Clara's article at the back of the issue, she'd changed the headline, replacing "Knitwits" with "Knitting Club." And she'd cut out two entire paragraphs!

Clara felt her cheeks flush, and she pushed the newspaper toward Lina, beginning to rethink her plan to send it to Elaine in West Palm Beach. If Wesley hadn't cared for her article, Elaine likely wouldn't either.

Back before she'd retired from her job as a government statistician, Elaine used to start each day the same way: with dry toast, black coffee and the *Toronto Times*. Clara would sit across the table from her, and Elaine would read her the latest news—but only the articles that presented cold, hard facts. Elaine was not one for, say, arts and entertainment.

Sometimes Clara's mother, Gaby, would listen in as she made her daily Super Soothing Lavender Smoothie. But Gaby was only really interested in the horoscopes, which made Elaine roll her eyes. Which in turn made Gaby whisper to Clara: "She's such a Virgo."

At which point Clara usually left the room.

No, she decided as the Newsies handed their papers back to the editor-in-chief, who slid them back in her briefcase: this was not the issue to send her grandmother. Hopefully the November issue would be better. Hopefully next time, Wesley would deem Clara to have proven her chops, and she'd give her a hard-hitting investigative piece.

She crossed her fingers that this was how things worked at the Kensington Middle School *Gazette*.

CHAPTER 2

"OH MY GOSH, CLARA, THE PLAY sounds AMAZING." Maeve Healy-Lin grabbed Clara's arm and squeezed it hard.

"Ow!" Clara winced. For someone roughly the size of a pixie, Maeve had surprising strength.

"Sorry." Maeve released her. "But I'm just so excited!" They paused at the edge of Dundas Street and waited for a streetcar to rumble by before hurrying across, alongside grocery shoppers and other kids just released from school. It was a perfect October afternoon—sunny and toasty-warm, but not sticky-hot—which didn't particularly match Clara's mood, but she was trying her best to forget the *Gazette* meeting.

"Ms. Flynn had planned to do *Snow White* again this year, which would have been a total snore," Maeve said as she leaped over a flock of pigeons on the sidewalk. "But at the last minute, she changed her mind and went with . . . wait for it . . . ," she lowered her voice to a whisper, "*The Seventh Slipper: A Morris Mumford Mystery*. Have you heard of it?"

"Like, Morris Mumford from *The Morris Mumford Mystery Hour*?" Clara asked as she dodged a baby stroller. "Of course I've heard of it." She had, in fact, watched it with Elaine every Sunday evening at 8 o'clock sharp. Elaine was a big fan of Detective Morris Mumford.

"Really? That's great!" Maeve exclaimed. "I've only seen a few episodes, and to be honest, I didn't love them."

"No?" Clara asked, though she wasn't really surprised.

Maeve shook her head. "They were just . . . just . . ." —she stroked an imaginary Morris Mumford mustache— "so *civilized*."

Clara nodded. That was exactly why Elaine liked Detective Mumford—that and the fact that he solved all his mysteries using only his powers of logic and analysis. Maeve, on the other hand, preferred mysteries that involved serial killers, car chases and the odd haunted house. She claimed to have watched nearly every crime drama ever made, and Clara believed it.

"Anyway," Maeve went on as they continued down the sidewalk, "at first I thought I'd just try out for one of the minor roles, like the chambermaid found poisoned in the library." She crossed her arms over her heart and offered her best impression of a dead chambermaid.

"Nice," Clara commented.

"Thanks." Maeve resumed her normal, conscious state. "But then I remembered that thing your mom likes to say."

Clara raised an eyebrow. "What thing?"

Maeve spread her arms wide. "Follow your bliss!" she cried. "And I think my bliss lies in playing the lead role:

Detective Morris Mumford himself! I know it's only my first audition, but I figure, why not?"

"Why not," Clara agreed, forcing a smile.

"We'll follow our bliss!" That's what her mother had declared back in June, a few days after Elaine had announced she was retiring and moving to West Palm Beach, Florida. Clara and Gaby had been stunned; they'd lived with Elaine ever since Clara was born, and not once had she mentioned wanting to retire, let alone move to Florida.

Once they'd recovered from the shock, Clara and Gaby turned their heads to practical matters, like where they would live. Clara had assumed they'd stay put in Elaine's little duplex in High Park, the only house she'd ever lived in. It wouldn't be nearly as clean and orderly without her grandmother in charge, but they'd manage somehow. Gaby had just finished her college herbalism program and was looking for work, so at least they wouldn't starve.

Her mother, however, had other plans.

"It's time for us to strike out on our own, Cee," she'd informed Clara. "We're going to forge our own path! We'll follow our bliss!"

"Follow our bliss?" Clara had a bad feeling about this. She loved her mother, but their notions of bliss were very different, though not quite as different as those of Elaine and Gaby. Gaby lived for impromptu adventures, while surprises gave Elaine hives. Gaby loved meeting new people; Elaine refused to answer the door if she didn't know the caller (and sometimes even if she did).

Clara fell somewhere in between. She enjoyed her mother's impromptu adventures, like the time they'd rented a car and gone camping at Long Beach (but ended up forgetting the camp stove and dining at an ice cream stand for two days). But she also liked returning home to Elaine's clean and orderly duplex—not to mention its well-stocked fridge. Sometimes, she believed, returning home was the best part of an adventure.

"Yes." Gaby had nodded firmly. "We're following our bliss. And do you know where our bliss lives?"

Clara wasn't sure she wanted to.

"Kensington Market!"

That's what Clara had been afraid of. Kensington Market was a good half-hour journey—by subway *and* streetcar—from High Park. It might as well have been in another country.

"Can't we just stay here?" Clara had asked, trying to stay calm in the face of this disastrous news. "We could buy the duplex off Elaine. Then we wouldn't have to pack. Remember how much you *hate* packing?"

Gaby shook her head. "We can't afford this place. Elaine is going to put it on the market next week. Don't worry about the packing—we don't own much stuff anyway. It'll be so much fun to start a new life, just you and me!"

Fun was not the word Clara would have chosen for starting a new life with her mother in Kensington Market.

Maeve was still talking about the play as they turned onto Kensington Avenue, and Clara tried to tune back in and ignore the knot forming at the back of her throat. It usually arose at this point in her walk home, when she stepped into the Market and suddenly the sun felt hotter and noises seemed louder and High Park, with its quiet, leafy streets, felt so much farther away.

"The problem is there are tons of other kids auditioning," Maeve was saying. "You should have seen the auditorium today: it was standing-room only. And some kids have real acting experience. Clara." She reached again for Clara's arm, but Clara withdrew it just in time. "Some kids have been *on TV.*"

"Really?"

"Really. This eighth grade girl, Emma Something-or-other, has been in a laundry detergent commercial! You know the one with all the kittens?"

Clara shook her head. She and her mother didn't have a TV in their new place.

"You'd know it to see it," Maeve assured her. "And then there's Jin—he hosts his own web series about dinosaurs. He'll definitely want to be Detective Mumford." She sighed. "How can I compete?"

"You can compete because you're a natural," Clara told her. And she wasn't just saying it because they were best friends. Maeve was literally born to be onstage: her mother had been a theater actress in London, England, before moving to Toronto to teach drama at the university. Though she'd never actually been in a play before, Maeve had been watching them since before she could walk. She'd nail this audition. Clara just knew it.

"*And* one of the girls is a model!" Maeve said as they passed the old purple house that sold secondhand clothes, like Gaby's favorite flowy cotton skirts. She owned at least a dozen, patterned with things like elephants, rainbows and constellations.

"Is that Olivia Silva?" Clara asked, remembering the "School Snaps" column and the sheepdog coat.

"The *KMS Fashionista*?" Maeve laughed. "No, she can't act. Haven't you watched her videos?"

Clara shook her head. Though Maeve was also in sixth grade, she already knew a ton of kids at KMS, having gone to elementary school close by. Ever since they'd met on the second day of school, Maeve had been trying to explain the lay of the land to her: who was friends with whom, who couldn't stand whom, who had significant social media followings and who only thought they did. But Clara still found it all overwhelming.

"You're not missing anything," Maeve assured her. Then she stopped, placed a hand on her hip and pursed her lips. "Today I'm modeling a dress I made just this morning, from the pillowcase I slept on last night," she said. "It takes no time at all when you're born with a sense of style. Also, check out my shoes."

Clara laughed. Maeve's impression was bang-on. "There's a profile of her in the October *Gazette*," she said.

No sooner had the words left her mouth than she remembered Wesley's warning not to talk about the paper: *You can't even tell your best friend.*

But did it really matter? Clara wondered. They were producing a middle-school newspaper—not the *Toronto Times*. And also, weren't best friends supposed to tell each other everything? She wasn't entirely sure, since she'd never had one before Maeve. But it sounded right.

"That was supposed to be top secret," she added. "Promise you won't tell?"

"Oh, absolutely!" Maeve crossed her heart. "I am an excellent secret keeper, Clara. One time in third grade, Bianca Esposito really, *really* had to go, and she didn't make it to the bathroom in time and, well, you get the picture. But I helped her hide the evidence under a sweater tied around her waist, and I swore I wouldn't tell a soul—that I'd take her secret to the grave! Well, until now, I guess," Maeve added. "Hey, don't tell Bianca, okay?"

"I don't know who Bianca is," said Clara.

"That works." Maeve grinned. They continued on into the Market.

"So did you see your article in print?" Maeve asked, as they passed a lime-green house that had been converted into an antique shop and a pea-green house that sold used books. "Was it so exciting? I can't wait to see it. I'll get, like, seventeen copies!"

"Oh." Clara frowned. "Um, maybe don't. Wesley changed a bunch of things in the article. It's not very good anymore."

"I bet it's better than you think," Maeve said. "Anyway, it was a snoozer of an assignment. She's bound to give you a better one next time."

"I hope so." Clara sighed.

"She will," said Maeve. "She has to let you prove your chips!"

"You mean chops," said Clara.

"Chips, chops." Maeve shrugged. "Hey, look at that guy's hat!" She pointed across the street.

Clara looked. On the sidewalk opposite them, a young man was striding along, with grocery bags in each hand and a top hat on his head. It wasn't entirely out of the ordinary for Kensington Market; in the past few months, Clara had seen many impressive outfits, including several pairs of fluorescent-striped leggings and star-shaped sunglasses. Once she'd even seen an actual cape.

"Don't stare." She tugged on Maeve's sleeve.

"Should we go ask where he got it?"

"No!" Clara cried. "Are you kidding?"

"Oh, come on," Maeve said, watching the man walk away. "It might make a good detective hat. I could use it for my audition." But she let Clara pull her on. "I love the Market," she said as they passed the cheese shop that, according to its sign, sold 22 KINDS OF GOUDA! "You're so lucky to live here."

"I'd trade with you any day," said Clara. Maeve lived just outside the Market, in a beautiful three-story brick house. It was only a fifteen-minute walk from Clara and Gaby's apartment, but it felt like an entire continent away.

Maeve didn't seem to hear. "Ooh, look." She pointed to a sign in a shop window. "Tarot card readings. Fifteen minutes for ten dollars!" she read. "Want to go in?"

"No." Clara pulled her on again. Walking home with Maeve always took five times as long as it ought to.

"But tarot cards tell your fortune! Don't you want to know your fortune?"

"No," Clara said again. All she wanted was to go home, close the door tight and shut out the Market for the day. Possibly Elaine would be free; it felt like ages since they'd last talked on the phone.

"Wait, you don't like having your fortune told?" Maeve ground to a halt once more. "Don't you want to know what the future has in store? Maybe the tarot reader could tell you if you're going to be a successful journalist! I mean, of course you are," she added hastily. "Like, totally. But don't you want to know for sure?"

Clara rolled her eyes. "It's not like that stuff is real. It's just woo."

"It's just what?"

"Woo," Clara repeated. "You know."

Maeve shook her head.

"It's woo-woo!" Clara waved her hands at the sky, like Elaine often did when she said it.

Maeve waved her hands at the sky as well. "Woo-woo?"

"You know!" Now Clara was getting impatient. "Fortune-telling and magic and witchcraft. It's all woo. It's not real."

"Woo," Maeve repeated. Then she laughed. "Woo-woo!" She waved her hands at the sky again. "I love it! Is that a Wesley Ferris word?"

Clara shook her head. "Elaine used to say it. My grandmother," she added, in case Maeve had forgotten.

"Toronto's Capital of Woo"—that's what Elaine used to call Kensington Market. It was her least favorite neighborhood in the entire city. When Clara was small, Gaby would take her on Saturday morning Market excursions in search of cheap produce, secondhand books and her flowy, patterned skirts. Elaine always refused to join them, and when they returned, she'd insist on inspecting everything they'd bought. Because Kensington Market, according to Elaine, was also Toronto's Capital of Bedbugs.

Maeve giggled. "I wish I'd met her before she moved away."

Clara nodded, though secretly she knew it was better this way. Elaine had discouraged her from inviting even her quietest and cleanest friends over to play. Maeve wouldn't have stood a chance.

"Let's go visit her someday," Maeve suggested as they passed the pasta shop that piped the same three Frank Sinatra songs out into the street all day. She launched into a tap dance on the sidewalk. "I mean, when we're old enough to travel by ourselves. We'll hop a plane to West Palm Beach and go surfing and . . . and have drinks with little umbrellas in them! Oh my gosh, Clara, it'll be so fun!" She spun on her toes.

Clara agreed: it did sound like fun. But the thought of waiting until she was grown-up to visit Elaine made her chest hurt. "Come on," she said, dragging Maeve on again.

She stopped when they reached the crooked steps of

Healing Herbs. "Well, I'll see you tomor—"

"I don't have to be home right away," Maeve said quickly. "I'll come in and hang out for a while."

"Oh." Clara glanced at the shop. The energy crystals Gaby had hung in the window gleamed in the sunlight. "Um, I'm not sure . . ."

"I am. I love your mom's shop. Ooh, maybe she'll make us some of that calendula tea again. Remember? The stuff that enhances psychic powers?"

"Oh, I remember." Clara sighed. It was exactly the kind of situation she wanted to avoid.

"Come on." Maeve nudged her toward the steps.

Clara hesitated a moment longer, wondering if refusing would be a bad best-friend move. She had a lot to learn about that too. She'd had friends at High Park Public, of course, but it was hard to reach best friend status when her grandmother wouldn't let them in the house. In that sense, she supposed, her new life was an improvement. But she'd still take her old life over—

"Cla-raaa, come onnn." Maeve pretended to snore.

"Okay, okay." Clara sighed. Then she turned, steeled herself and led the way up the steps to Healing Herbs.

CHAPTER 3

GABY COSTA WAS HARD AT WORK, concocting an herbal remedy.

"Mmm." Maeve sniffed the air like a bloodhound as the door swung shut behind them. "I smell lavender. And maybe . . . chamomile?"

Clara sniffed. "Mugwort." She hung her backpack on a hook near the door. She still wasn't sure what mugwort was, exactly, but lately her mother had been tossing it in everything, from smoothies to spaghetti sauce. It definitely didn't belong in spaghetti sauce.

"Hi, girls!" Gaby looked up from her mixing bowl. "Come join us. I'm just whipping up a treatment for Paquito." She smiled at the man sitting on a stool across the counter from her.

Paquito tipped his Blue Jays cap at Clara. "Your mom thinks she can cure me."

Clara joined him at the counter. She liked Paquito, who owned the taco shop across the street (aptly named Paquito's). He had a shy but friendly smile, and he tried to know all his customers by name. But best of all, he seemed, well, *normal*. At least compared to the other friends Gaby had made since moving to the Market. The last new friend she'd made, for instance, had come over for dinner and insisted on rearranging all their furniture "for better flow of energy."

"What's wrong?" Clara climbed up on a stool next to him, and Maeve hopped onto one beside hers.

"I'm a total insomniac." Paquito sighed. "I haven't had a good night's sleep in a week."

Gaby clucked sympathetically as she slid a mixture of herbs from her big mixing bowl into a smaller stone bowl, which she called a mortar. She began to crush the herbs with a blunt stone tool called a pestle.

"I've tried everything," Paquito went on. "Chamomile tea, counting backwards from a hundred, deep breathing . . . I even read an entire book on stamp-collecting!"

"Yikes," said Clara. She wondered if perhaps he'd like a go at her knitting club article.

"Seriously," said Paquito. "Without sleep, my taco game slips. And the people need their tacos!" He lifted his cap to wipe the sweat from his bald head, then set it back down.

This *was* a real concern. Paquito made the very best tacos in Kensington Market, which was really saying something, since there were five taco shops within four blocks of Healing Herbs. But Paquito's had the freshest ingredients, and his guacamole was to die for. Clara and Gaby devoured a small bucket of it every Friday night—practically their combined weight, as Gaby liked to say.

"Don't you worry," Gaby told him. "This philter is going to do the trick. I just know it."

"What's a philter?" asked Maeve.

"It's a combination of herbs and liquid," said Gaby. "It can come in many forms. In this case, Paquito will put these herbs in fresh water and simmer them for thirty minutes. Then he'll drink it down."

"Wow," Maeve breathed, watching her crush the herbs. "It's like magic."

"No, it isn't," Clara said quickly. "Plants really do have healing properties—they're even used in modern medicines. It's more like science," she assured Paquito, who seemed like a reasonable person. Fortunately, he didn't appear to be creeped out.

Gaby slid the contents of her bowl into a little paper bag. "Also, Paquito, keep in mind that Mercury is in retrograde right now. Trust me, you're not the only sleepless one these days."

Clara sighed. At least, *part* of her mother's work was like science.

"What does that mean?" asked Maeve.

"It has to do with the alignment of the planets." Gaby waved a hand vaguely at the ceiling. "For the next three weeks, nothing we do is going to go as planned. It's the worst time of year. You really have to protect yourself."

Clara shook her head. She knew exactly what Elaine would say to that: "Woo!"

She didn't say it herself, though. Her mother hated that word.

Gaby handed Paquito his remedy. "After you've simmered the herbs, strain out the liquid and drink it straight away. But keep the steeped herbs and simmer them again the next night for an extra dose. You'll be sleeping like a baby after that, I promise."

"I hope so," said Paquito. He thanked her, bade them goodbye and hurried out, back to the people who needed their tacos.

"Well, that was fun!" Gaby put her hands on her hips and drew herself up tall, like Wonder Woman, but in a lime-green Healing Herbs apron.

"You forgot to charge him," Clara pointed out.

"What?" Her mother gasped. "Oh no!" She spun toward the door, but Paquito had already disappeared into his restaurant across the street. "Shoot." Her shoulders sagged. "I'm so forgetful these days."

"Maybe it's Mercury in retrograde," Maeve suggested.

"Oh, good call." Gaby pointed at her. Maeve grinned.

Clara sighed. It was extremely tiresome, being the only one who didn't buy into the woo.

"Oh well, Paquito's a friend," Gaby said, wiping bits of lavender and mugwort off the counter. "I'm sure he'll pay next time."

Clara wasn't sure the owner of Healing Herbs would agree, but fortunately, he was rarely around. He left the shop management entirely to Gaby, although she'd never managed a shop—or anything else—before. In fact, she'd rarely had a job for more than a few months at a time, though she'd certainly tried a lot of them over the years, while saving up to go back to school. Once, Elaine had convinced the owners of a fancy clothing shop in High Park to hire her, but Gaby was deemed "not a good fit" after encouraging one of the customers to wear an expensive silk scarf as a skirt. Another time, she'd lost her job as a gardener for refusing to pluck out weeds, which she argued were just as attractive as the flowers.

"So, have you noticed anything different?" her mother asked.

Clara looked her up and down. Gaby's long, dark hair—identical to Clara's own—was pulled back in its usual smooth ponytail, and her favorite earrings—clusters of shooting stars—dangled from her ears.

"New skirt?" Maeve asked.

Clara shook her head. Gaby had owned the skirt patterned with technicolor swirls for years. Elaine had "accidentally" garbaged it a few times, but Gaby always found it and fished it out of the bin.

"We give up," said Clara. "What's new?"

Gaby spun to face the wall behind her, whose shelves were crammed with jars of herbs. She spread her arms wide. "Ta-da! I rearranged everything!"

"You did?" Clara squinted at the herbs, which had always lined the shelves in alphabetical order. It was Clara's job, actually, to make sure that they were properly arranged at the end of every day. "How?"

"By planetary connection!" Gaby grabbed a book from behind the counter. "I got the idea from *Herbal Alchemy*.

Remember this book, Cee? It really changed everything for me. I'm so glad I found it. Actually," she added, hugging it to her chest, "I kind of feel like it found me."

"It didn't," Clara informed her. "I was there. You pulled it off the shelf."

"How does it work?" Maeve wanted to know.

Ignoring Clara's comment, Gaby smiled at Maeve. "Well, according to *Herbal Alchemy*, each healing herb is connected with the energy of a planet."

"Planets have energies?" asked Clara, who was pretty sure they didn't.

Gaby nodded. "There's a whole body of research behind this, dating back to the fourteenth century. Anyway," she went on quickly, before Clara could question these fourteenth-century research methods, "I've arranged my herbs accordingly." She hopped over to the right side of the wall. "Here, we have the herbs of the sun—"

"Which isn't a planet," Clara pointed out.

"Hmm, that's true." Her mother frowned, and then shrugged. "Herbs of the sun include calendula, eyebright, juniper and many more. They're connected with success, self-confidence and courage. Next, we have herbs of the moon—they're all about psychic knowledge and dreaming. Then we have herbs of Mercury, Venus, Mars and so on."

"That's so cool!" Maeve cried.

"I think so too." Gaby grinned. "And I've started to see patterns in people's herbal needs. For example, with Mercury in retrograde right now, people are feeling pretty unbalanced.

So I'm making all kinds of remedies with my herbs of Saturn, which make you feel grounded and stable. I've even had to order extra patchouli and wolfsbane!"

"Imagine that," Clara said dryly.

Maeve stroked an imaginary Morris Mumford mustache again. "I think this whole Mercury thing explains a lot," she said. "Think about it, Clara: maybe that's why you ended up with a boring *Gazette* assignment. Maybe it's Mercury's fault that—"

But before she could finish her theory, and before Clara could refute it, the bell on the door jangled and in walked a woman about Gaby's age. She had short black curls and wore a long black lace dress paired with white gloves that reached past her elbows.

"Welcome to Healing Herbs!" Gaby chirped. "How can I help you?"

"Oh, I *hope* you can help me," the woman sighed. "I've been so forgetful lately—my brain is a sieve."

"I've got just what you need!" Gaby spun to face her wall of herbs. "A mixture of boneset, yew and patchouli will do just the—oh."

"What's wrong?" asked the woman.

"I'm almost out of patchouli." Gaby held up a near-empty jar of shriveled, greenish-brown leaves. "It's a herb of Saturn, which everyone needs right now."

"Oh no." The woman looked crestfallen.

"Wait!" Gaby snapped her fingers. "I think I have some upstairs. I was using it last night for a bath soak. Remember, Cee?"

Clara remembered it well; she'd had to open her bedroom window to keep her school clothes from stinking like patchouli. She still didn't know much about KMS, but she was fairly certain that would spell social suicide.

"Can you run up and grab it? It's in the bathroom by the sink."

"Sure." Clara slid off her stool, happy to escape.

"I'll come!" Maeve hopped off hers too.

"Oh." Clara paused. "Don't worry, I can find it myself."

"I'm not worried." Maeve laughed. "I want to come."

"Right, but . . . Don't you want to watch?" She waved at her mother, who was plucking herbs of Saturn off the wall.

"Nope," said Maeve. "I want to see your apartment again. You only let me in that one time, and I love it *so* much."

Well, that makes one of us, thought Clara.

"Cee?" said Gaby. "I'm kind of in a hurry here. Can you hustle?"

"Okay, okay." She headed for the back of the shop, with Maeve close behind. They walked through the storeroom, past shelves lined with boxes and dusty old books, and then took the stairs up to the second floor.

"This reminds me of the crime show my dad and I watched last night," Maeve said as they climbed the steps. "These two detectives were searching for a serial killer in this creepy old abandoned shop."

Clara shivered. She'd take "civilized" Morris Mumford mysteries over crime dramas any day. The few times Maeve had insisted they watch them together, she'd spent a good part of the time hiding in the bathroom, waiting for the scary parts to end.

The hallway at the top of the stairs smelled sour, as usual. She considered switching on the light overhead, but that would only highlight the yellow stains on the walls. Gaby kept promising to paint them—she swore she could make the hallway look more inviting. Clara would believe that when she saw it.

"I think it was a pharmacy," Maeve went on, "or maybe a hardware shop? Anyway, there was a little apartment above it, just like yours, except no one had been up there for years. And Clara!" She dropped her voice to a whisper. "Do you want to know what they found?"

"I'd rather not," said Clara.

"*A dead body!*"

"Great, thanks." Clara unlocked the apartment door and pushed it open. "I'm never sleeping again."

Maeve laughed. "Oh, the beaded curtain!" She wrapped herself in the strings of beads that hung in the doorway. "This is my favorite part of your—Clara!" She gasped. "You painted the kitchen!"

"My *mom* painted the kitchen." Clara stepped inside without taking off her sneakers, which she would never have dreamed of doing when they lived with Elaine. It only took a dozen steps to pass through the kitchen and living room and into the bathroom. She grabbed the patchouli and turned to go.

But Maeve was wandering around the kitchen, her green

eyes wide. "I didn't even know paint existed in this color! I wish my house looked like this!"

"No, you don't," Clara said, herding her toward the door. The Healy-Lin house had furniture that actually matched and radiators that worked without needing to be kicked. And it didn't have a family of squirrels nesting in the roof—Clara could hear them now, scampering around above her head. It made her skin crawl. Elaine would never have tolerated squirrels nesting in her roof.

"I really do," Maeve insisted, spinning in a circle with her arms spread wide. "You're so lucky to live here."

Clara opened her mouth, and then shut it. Arguing about the apartment was as tiring as arguing about the woo.

"The universe is providing, Cee!" That's what her mother had declared when they'd visited it for the very first time, back in July. "An apartment right upstairs from my new workplace? How lucky are we?"

"We're actually going to *live here*?" Clara had felt faint as she wandered from room to room, taking in the dusty windows and the low, slanted ceilings. They were so low and slanted that the bathroom couldn't even house a stand-up shower. Elaine would have lost her mind.

"You bet we are," her mother had said. And she'd thrown herself into cleaning and painting and furnishing the apartment with stuff she'd found at yard sales (and a few pieces that Clara suspected she'd found in the dumpster out back, like the kitchen chairs that wobbled and swayed when you sat on them, as if they were about to pass out).

The kitchen had been the last room she'd painted—her "pièce de résistance," she'd called it. Once she'd finished, she insisted Clara call Elaine in West Palm Beach and give her a virtual tour on the laptop.

"What is that *color*?" Elaine had shrieked when Clara pointed the laptop at the kitchen wall.

"It's called Ripe Tomato, Mom!" Gaby had called over Clara's shoulder. "Isn't it vibrant?"

"It looks like a crime scene!" cried Elaine. "And . . . good Lord, is that the *bathroom*?"

"It's called Mango Tango," Clara told her.

"I'm dizzy just looking at it," said Elaine. "And I'm not even there!"

Clara wanted to tell her that it was even worse in the morning, when you stumbled in to brush your teeth, only to find yourself trapped inside the flesh of a tropical fruit. But she didn't, because Gaby had spent the past two months agonizing over paint colors. After years of living in a land of neutrals, she claimed, she was desperate for color. Her own bedroom was now Peacock Blue, the living room Electric Purple. Clara's room had the only white walls in the entire apartment, but she knew it was only a matter of time until she came home to find her mother slathering them in Mega Magenta or Shamrock Green.

"Come on, let's go." Clara pushed Maeve back out through the beaded curtain and down to the shop, where Gaby and her customer were chatting away like old friends. Clara handed over the patchouli, and Gaby added it to her concoction.

"I call this a tea bath," she told the woman. "You'll draw yourself a nice, hot bath and then toss in these herbs. Let them steep for fifteen minutes at least, and then hop in and soak for as long as possible. You should start feeling sharper almost immediately." She poured the herbs into a small bag and handed them over.

"This is so great," the woman gushed. "Thank you, sweet pea. I'm so glad we met." She paid for her remedy and sashayed out of the shop.

"Sweet pea?" Clara wrinkled her nose.

Gaby grinned. "Isn't she cool? We're totally going to be friends. You know when you meet someone and you just *know*?"

Maeve nodded vigorously. "That's exactly how it was with me and Clara. Best friends at first sight!"

Clara nodded too, though it wasn't really true for her. Maeve had ambushed her at her locker on the second day of school, demanding to know where Clara had bought her T-shirt, which featured a *Wizard of Oz* show poster.

"That's my favorite movie ever!" Maeve had declared.

Secretly, Clara had never cared much for *The Wizard of Oz*, though she did find the defeat of the Wicked Witch highly satisfying. She'd pulled on the T-shirt at the last minute that morning, after staining her first-choice shirt with the Super Soothing Lavender Smoothie Gaby had made her.

Maeve had insisted Clara take her to the secondhand shop where she'd found it, so they'd stopped in the next day after school. And though they didn't find another *Wizard of Oz*

T-shirt, Maeve had scored a feather boa, which pleased her immensely. By the end of the week, they were best friends. "For life," according to Maeve.

"Her name is Lily," Gaby went on as she wiped down the counter again. "She and her husband live just down the street. Apparently Lily can read tea leaves, so we'll have her over for brunch someday, and she'll tell us our fortunes. Doesn't that sound amazing, Cee?"

Clara had a lot of words for that scenario, but *amazing* wasn't one of them.

"Can I come too?" Maeve begged. "They sound so cool. All my parents' friends are so normal."

"You have no idea how lucky you are," Clara muttered.

"What's that?" Maeve and Gaby asked in unison.

"Nothing," Clara said with a sigh, outnumbered as usual.

And once again, she missed her grandmother.

CHAPTER 4

"I HAVE A SURPRISE FOR YOU!"

Maeve declared first thing Friday morning, when she appeared beside Clara's locker.

Clara shoved her lunch bag, which reeked like the previous night's dinner of lentil-mugwort loaf, deep into the recesses of her locker. She shut the door quickly, making a mental note not to let Gaby pack her lunch again ever. "What is it?" she asked casually, hoping Maeve couldn't smell the lentils.

Maeve was bouncing from one sneaker to the other, her hands behind her back. "Want to guess? No, I can't wait." She whipped out a box roughly the size of a generous slice of lentil-mugwort loaf. "Happy friendiversary!"

"Happy what?" Clara took the box, which was stamped with a big gold *S*. "Whoa. Is this from Sammy's?"

"Yes, yes, yes!" Maeve squealed. "My dad and I stopped in on the way to school."

"Wow!" Sammy's was a fancy new doughnut shop on College Street, just a few blocks away from Maeve's house.

According to Gaby, a couple of Sammy's doughnuts cost as much as she'd paid to furnish their entire living room. Clara didn't doubt it.

She opened the box and peeked inside at the pillowy pastry, expertly dusted in sugar. She felt like she was holding a rare gem. "Thank you! But . . . why?"

"It's our one-month friendiversary," Maeve explained. "Remember? We met exactly one month ago today."

"We did?" said Clara. "I mean, of course we did," she added hastily, though she'd completely forgotten and had never even heard of a friendiversary. "Um, I . . . didn't get you anything. I'm sorry." She shut the box, feeling like a failed friend. Who knew that friendiversaries were even a thing? She had so much to learn.

"That's okay." Maeve shrugged.

"Let's split it." Clara opened the box again and pulled out the doughnut.

"Well, if you insist." Maeve grinned.

"Happy friendiversary," Clara said as they walked to first-period science class, licking sugar off their fingers.

"Happy friendiversary," Maeve returned. "I was thinking—"

"Quiet! We're filming!"

They looked up from their fingers.

"Get out of the way!" snapped an older girl holding a video camera. "We're shooting here!"

They leaped out of the way, and then stopped to survey the scene. In the middle of the hallway stood Olivia Silva, this time wearing a white dress that appeared to have been made from party streamers.

Olivia flashed a toothy smile at the camera. "Today on *KMS Fashionista*, I'm interviewing a special guest. He's a talented photographer with a great sense of style. Everyone, meet Preston Paisley!" She stepped aside, and Preston strolled over, with his camera around his neck and his thumbs tucked into a pair of red suspenders.

"Oh, gag," Maeve whispered.

"Welcome, Preston." Olivia smiled down at him. "Let's talk about your unique sense of style. Where did you get those—"

"*What's going on here?*" a voice bellowed, bringing the entire hallway to a halt. Even the teachers heading to class froze in mid-stride, clutching their coffee mugs.

"It's her!" Maeve gasped.

Before anyone could scatter or take cover, Mrs. Major, the custodian, came barreling around the corner, fists pumping. Roughly the size of a professional linebacker, with biceps as big as five-pin bowling balls, Mrs. Major had cold gray eyes and wispy sand-colored hair, which she slicked back in a bun and pinned into submission.

"What's going on here?" she demanded again.

Everyone turned to Olivia for the answer. Preston slipped behind her for cover.

"W-we're just shooting a video, Mrs. Major," she said, tugging at her streamer skirt. "For *KMS Fashionista*. That's my YouTube series."

Mrs. Major blinked at her furiously. "You're blocking the hall! Did you have a permit for this?"

"A permit?" Olivia glanced at the girl with the video camera. "Did you get a permit?" she hissed. The girl shook her head, and Olivia gave her a murderous look. "Sorry, Mrs. Major," she said, turning back to the custodian. "We'll be really quick, I prom—"

"Wait." Mrs. Major's head swiveled, like an owl spotting its prey. Her gray eyes zeroed in on Preston's bowling shoes. "Are those . . . ," she looked down at him, "outdoor shoes?"

Preston opened his mouth, and then shut it.

"I just waxed the floor!" she bellowed.

"Come on." Maeve tugged on Clara's sleeve. "Let's get out of here." They hurried off to science class.

"Whoa," Clara breathed once they were safely out of earshot. "I've never been that close to her before. She's terrifying!"

"I know, right?" said Maeve, glancing back. "I sure wouldn't want to be Preston right now. I heard she once tackled a kid for tracking mud onto her freshly waxed floors."

"No way," Clara said, though she could totally picture it.

Maeve nodded. "He had to wear a neck brace for a week."

Clara shuddered. Of all the things she'd had to adjust to since the summer, the KMS custodian was up there with the most unsettling. At High Park Public, the school custodian was an older man who rarely said a word, and he definitely didn't stand guard at the cafeteria recycling station during lunchtime, threatening detention for anyone who contaminated the paper bin with plastic.

"I can do a mean Mrs. Major imitation, you know," Maeve said as they sat down side by side in Ms. Thien's classroom. "Oh, speaking of imitations, want to help me rehearse for my audition tomorrow?"

"Sure," said Clara. It was really the least she could do, having forgotten their friendiversary.

Science class had barely begun when someone knocked loudly on the classroom door.

Clara sat up straight—she'd been replaying the scene with Mrs. Major in the hallway, marveling at the size of the custodian's muscles. But she relaxed when Mr. Devlin, the principal, walked in. There was nothing scary about Mr. Devlin. He talked to all the kids in the hallway, wore colorful Hawaiian shirts on Fridays and even led school cheers at basketball games. He was pretty well the polar opposite of Mrs. Major.

"Hi, Mr. Devlin!" a few kids called out.

"Hi, guys," he said. "Ms. Thien, can I have a moment with the class?"

"Go right ahead." The science teacher gave him the floor.

Mr. Devlin folded his hands in front of his Hawaiian shirt, which today featured frolicking flamingos. "Sorry to interrupt, everyone, but I have an important announcement. And . . . ," he paused, "it's a serious one."

The students exchanged curious glances. Clara looked over at Maeve, who raised her eyebrows and stroked an imaginary mustache.

"Yesterday evening, a crime took place at KMS."

The class gasped.

Mr. Devlin nodded. "A serious one. I never thought I'd hear myself say these words, but . . ." He drew a breath. "Someone has stolen Buzzter the Honeybee."

"Buzzter?" someone in the back row repeated.

"Buzzter!" Maeve clasped her hands over her heart.

"You mean the mascot?" asked Clara.

Mr. Devlin nodded grimly. "Our school mascot. The embodiment of our school spirit."

"Like, the papier-mâché bee," Clara said, just to be sure.

Maeve nodded vigorously. "The one and only."

"Needless to say, I am gutted." Mr. Devlin bowed his head. "I can't imagine why anyone would do such a thing."

Clara couldn't imagine it either, and not just because stealing was a crime. Buzzter the Honeybee was ugly. Really ugly.

According to KMS legend (which Clara had heard from Lina Gagliano), Buzzter had been born in an eighth grade art class over ten years before, when some kids decided to make a piñata shaped like a bee. They'd filled his belly with old Halloween candy and painted him with black-and-purple stripes, since the art room was low on yellow paint. Then they'd glued two creepy googly eyes on his lumpy head and named him Buzzter.

For reasons Clara couldn't fathom, the kids had decided that they liked Buzzter too much to whack him with a base-ball bat for the sake of the Tootsie Rolls in his belly. Instead, they knotted a yellow tie around his neck and petitioned the principal to make him the KMS mascot. Buzzter had lived in the school office ever since, perched on a podium near the door, where he could keep a googly eye on students who straggled in late or got caught eating ice cream in the Market when they should have been in class.

Of course, with a honeybee for a mascot, the school sports teams could no longer be called the Cowboys. Not that this was a great loss; there were clearly no cows in Toronto, and just as many girls played school sports as boys. But the KMS Honeybees didn't sound remotely intimidating, so after much debate, the staff settled on the KMS Hornets, even though Buzzter did not look remotely hornet-like.

It was all a rather complicated piece of KMS history.

"To add insult to injury, the thief left this behind." Mr. Devlin held up Buzzter's yellow necktie.

Maeve gasped. "No!"

"Yes." The principal nodded. "It might be the worst crime in the history of KMS. I have yet to decide what will happen to the thief when we find them."

"Put a price on their head!" Maeve declared.

"Maeve!" Clara shushed her.

Maeve shrugged. "Just a suggestion."

"If anyone has information about Buzzter's where-abouts, come see me or one of your teachers immediately. We want to ensure the safe return of our honeybee. Is that clear?"

Everyone nodded. Mr. Devlin thanked Ms. Thien, tucked Buzzter's necktie into his chest pocket and trudged back out. As soon as he was gone, everyone began talking at once.

"Now that," said Maeve, "is a great mystery. One for Detective Morris Mumford, I'd say." She tipped an imaginary hat at Clara. "Why would anyone steal a papier-mâché bee, but leave behind his necktie?"

"Also," Clara wondered, "do bees even *have* necks?"

Maeve shrugged. "Why does that matter?"

Clara shrugged back. "It's an important detail." Actually, it was the kind of thing Wesley Ferris would want the Newsies to investigate. Those little details that—

"Whoa," Clara said as it hit her. It was perfect. The disappearance of Buzzter the Honeybee would make an ideal investigative article for the KMS *Gazette*!

Especially if she could write it herself.

And to make a perfect opportunity even more perfect, Wesley would be handing out assignments for the November issue at noon that very day. This could be her chance to prove her chops!

There was no time to lose. She pulled out her notebook and started to plan.

CHAPTER 5

SHE THOUGHT ABOUT THE DISAPPEARANCE

of Buzzter the Honeybee all morning, considering who would steal an ugly old piñata, and why. Was it a student playing a prank? A disgruntled cafeteria worker? A desperate parent in need of a last-minute birthday party game?

Clara noted them all in her list of possible suspects and motives.

By lunchtime, she'd even come up with a solid lead, which was newspaper-speak for the opening lines of an article. According to Wesley, a lead had to grab the readers' attention and make them want to read on. Clara's lead went like this:

Who stole our honeybee? The students of Kensington Middle School are buzzing over the recent disappearance of their mascot.

It contained a pun, but a subtler one than "knitwits," which she could now admit had been a bit much.

When the lunch bell rang, Clara headed straight from French class to Mr. B.'s classroom for the Friday-lunch *Gazette* meeting. Wesley was already seated at the head of the table, and Clara noted with relief that she was not wearing a blazer, but a black cardigan over a white blouse.

"I have an idea!" she blurted before she could lose her nerve.

Wesley looked up from her laptop and blinked. "Sorry, what?"

"The mystery of the missing mascot!" Clara dropped into a chair beside her. "It would make an amazing investigative article. A perfect one, I think. And I'd really like to write it if—"

"Oh, I know," Wesley cut in. "I've got it on my list." She pointed to her laptop. "Don't worry. I'm on it."

"Um. Okay." Clara sat back in her chair, unsure what this meant. "But I'm wondering if I can write—"

"Let's talk about it later, okay?" Wesley flashed her a quick smile and then turned back to her laptop.

"Right. Sure," said Clara. She knew better than to pester her, even if it wasn't a Blazer Day. Wesley was very particular about assignments. For example, a Newsie couldn't just come up with an idea, write a story and hand it in without her approval. That, she'd explained at the first meeting of the year, was what editors called an "unsolicited article," and Wesley didn't approve of those.

"Okay, Newsies, listen up!" she called a few minutes later, once everyone had arrived. "We've got lots of important things to talk about today. First off, the October issue is now on stands! I delivered it myself first thing this morning, and I think it looks great."

She paused to flash a smile around the table and then continued. "Second, I've decided to make a change to our publishing schedule. From now on, we're going to produce not one, but *two* issues per month."

"Wait, what?" Lina dropped her pencil.

"We are?" The Newsies exchanged glances.

"We are," Wesley confirmed. "There's a lot going on at KMS these days, and students deserve to know about it all. More news is good news, you know."

"Isn't the saying '*No* news is good news'?" asked Lizzie.

"I'm pretty sure more news is more work," Sienna, a sports reporter, pointed out.

Wesley frowned. "Look, guys, I know it's a big change, but you're going to have to trust me. This will improve the quality of my—I mean, *our*—newspaper and the lives of all KMS students!"

"Not to mention the quality of her high school portfolio," Lina muttered, picking up her pencil. Clara shushed her.

"And Mr. B. supports it. Right, Mr. B.?" Wesley turned toward his desk.

Mr. B. looked up from the papers he'd been marking and blinked. "Sorry, what?"

"You support the new publishing schedule," Wesley informed him.

Mr. B. squinted, as if trying to remember what that meant. "Sure," he said.

"Exactly." Wesley turned back to the team. "So Newsies, this means your articles for our next issue are now due first thing Tuesday morning. You've got the weekend to finish them, plus I'll give you one extra day." She smiled graciously.

"Tuesday!" the Newsies buzzed.

"But you haven't even assigned them," Ravi pointed out.

"That's not enough time to create a comic!" cried Lina. "You can't rush art!"

"I know you guys can handle it." Wesley smiled at them. "Okay, moving on. I've made a full list of assignments for the next issue." She pulled some papers out of her briefcase.

Clara drew in a breath and crossed her fingers.

"Ravi, I'm giving you the forgery feature," Wesley told him.

"What's that?" Ravi leaned forward eagerly.

"Some kid has been writing fake sick notes and selling them for five dollars apiece," she explained. "It's driving all the teachers crazy. No one knows who the kid is, not even Mr. Devlin. It has good investigative potential."

"Cool." Ravi grinned.

Clara's stomach lurched. She would have *loved* to investigate forgery! She and Elaine had once watched an entire *Morris Mumford Mystery Hour* about it, wherein Detective Mumford tracked down an international counterfeit criminal just by using his powers of observation and handwriting analysis. Elaine had loved that one.

Wesley turned to Preston. "I thought you could profile Marcus Nilsson for your 'School Snaps' column. He's in sixth grade, and he just won a big cooking contest. I think he made a cheese soufflé."

"You want me to photograph a kid who cooks?" Preston curled his lip.

"He's going to be on The Food Channel," Wesley added.

"I'm on it!" Preston picked up his camera and began polishing the lens.

Clara gritted her teeth.

Wesley continued handing out assignments. Lina would create a comic strip about the new bike helmet rule, questioning whether being forced to wear a helmet to school was, as Wesley suggested, "an infringement on our personal rights and freedoms." Lizzie would continue to document the auditions for *The Seventh Slipper*, investigating whether the kids who claimed to be experienced actors did, in fact, have legitimate credits. And Matt and Sienna would report on the latest volleyball, basketball and field hockey games.

"I also got a last-minute request from Mrs. Major." Wesley frowned at her laptop. "She wants us to report on the dangers of contaminating the new green bins with garbage. Apparently some kids don't understand the basics of composting." She shrugged. "But I think we'll say no to that. Staff shouldn't be allowed to dictate newspaper content. It's undemocratic."

"You're going to say no to Mrs. Major?" Lizzie's eyes widened.

"Not even Mr. Devlin turns down a request from Mrs. Major," Ravi pointed out.

Wesley squared her shoulders and nodded. "I'm sure. And don't worry. If Mrs. Major has a problem with it, she can talk to me."

Though Clara doubted that would go well for Wesley, she was also relieved she wouldn't get stuck writing an article about composting.

But as the end of lunch drew closer, Clara began to wonder whether she would get an assignment at all. She felt her cheeks redden. The only thing worse than profiling the knitting club would be no assignment whatsoever.

But Wesley hadn't yet mentioned the Buzzter story, she reminded herself. So there was still hope. She kept her fingers tightly crossed.

Finally, at five minutes to one, Wesley set down her papers and glanced at her laptop. "Okay, guys. Let's talk about Buzzter the Honeybee."

"Oh yeah!" said Ravi. "That'll make the best investigative article! We have to write about Buzzter."

Clara sucked in her breath. Wesley *couldn't* give the assignment to Ravi. He already had a great story. It would be so unfair!

"Oh, we will," Wesley assured him.

Clara rallied her courage and raised her hand. "I can do it. I don't . . . have an assignment yet," she added, in case it had slipped Wesley's mind.

"Clara." Wesley looked at her as if she'd forgotten she existed. "Hmm."

Clara held her breath.

"I have something else in mind for you," said Wesley. "I'm going to give this assignment to Preston." She turned to him. "How does that sound, Preston? Are you up for a good investigative piece?"

Preston? Clara's mouth fell open. *Preston Paisley?* Preston wasn't even a writer!

Even Preston looked surprised. "Me?"

Wesley nodded. "It's going to involve a lot of investigation. Interviewing suspects, tracking down clues. Think you can do it?"

"Uh, I guess so," he said.

"It's a really important article," Wesley added. "I'll even give you until Wednesday to finish it."

Lina huffed at the injustice.

Preston picked up his fancy camera, pointed it across the table and snapped twice, for no good reason. "Yeah, sure. I'm on it. How hard can it be?"

Clara sat back, stunned. *How hard can it be?* It was the story of the year! She looked at Wesley, expecting her to launch into a lecture on the challenges of investigative journalism.

But Wesley had turned back to her laptop. "I think that's it then, Newsies. Oh wait." She looked up. "Clara. Sorry. I forgot about you. I've got an . . . interesting assignment for you too."

Clara tried to swallow her distress. "Okay. What is it?"

Wesley drummed her fingernails on her keyboard. "To be honest, I wasn't sure whether to include this—it's not my favorite part of a newspaper. But our readers have told me that it's important to them, and in the newspaper business, you really need to listen to your readers."

Clara waited.

Wesley paused, then nodded. "We'll just try it out. And if it doesn't go well, we'll adjust our strategy. In the newspaper business, you have to try new things, then evaluate their success and adjust your strategy."

"Great." Now Clara was dying to know. "So what is it?"

Wesley snapped her laptop shut. "You, Clara," she said, "are going to write the horoscopes."

CHAPTER 6

"HOROSCOPES?" MAEVE'S EYEBROWS
leaped up into her bangs.

"Horoscopes," Clara confirmed, pulling her backpack out of her locker, which still smelled like lentils and mugwort.

"Horoscopes," Maeve repeated in a whisper. Then she punched the air. "I LOVE horoscopes!" she declared.

"I know you do." Clara shut her locker and shouldered her backpack.

"I'm a Gemini, you know," said Maeve.

"Oh, I know." Clara sighed. The first time Maeve and Gaby had met, they'd quickly established that they were both Geminis. "Are you ready to go?" After what felt like one of the longest afternoons of her life, she couldn't wait to get home.

"Almost." Maeve waved at a group of girls passing by. "See you guys Monday!"

"Are you nervous?" one asked.

"*So* nervous!" said Maeve. "But Clara's helping me practice tomorrow. Right?" She elbowed Clara.

"Huh? Oh, sure." Clara had already forgotten about her promise.

"Great." Maeve studied the contents of her locker, then turned back to Clara. "Your birthday is July fifteenth, right? So that makes you . . ."

"A Cancer," Clara muttered. She'd always felt kind of shortchanged, getting stuck with the sign with the worst name. *Not* that she actually cared about horoscopes.

"You don't seem excited about your new assignment," Maeve observed.

"I am not excited about my new assignment," Clara agreed. "Can you hurry?"

"What's your new assignment?" Maddie Yuen, a friend of Maeve's from elementary school, popped up beside them.

Clara groaned inwardly. At this rate, she'd never get home.

"Clara's going to write horoscopes for the *Gazette*!" said Maeve.

"Horoscopes! That's totally what the *Gazette* is missing." Maddie held up a copy of the October issue. "Nice sewing club article, by the way."

"Knitting." Clara forced a smile through gritted teeth. "And thank you."

"I've got five copies!" Maeve patted her backpack. "One for each of my parents, and three for me."

"Great," said Clara. "Now can we leave?"

"I'm a Libra," Maddie told her. "Write me a good fortune, okay?"

"She will," Maeve promised. "What?" she asked when Clara gave her the stink-eye.

"Have a good weekend!" Maddie skipped off down the hall.

"Okay." Maeve slammed her locker door. "Let's get out of here."

"Finally!"

"So what do you have against horoscopes?" Maeve asked as they passed the office, headed for the front doors. "Oh, wait. I know." She waved her hands at the ceiling. "Woo!"

"Exactly," Clara said. They pushed open the front doors and let themselves out into another sunny afternoon. "But it's more than that," she added, and she filled Maeve in on the Buzzter debacle.

"Preston Paisley?" Maeve cried as they turned onto Kensington Avenue, which was packed with Friday afternoon shoppers. "But this is a serious crime! It requires an investigative journalist, and Wesley is sending in the . . . the paparazzi!" She shook her fist at the sky, nearly clocking a man passing by.

Clara nodded, shoving her own fists into her jacket pockets.

"I saw Preston's column." Maeve pulled a copy of the *Gazette* out of her backpack and flipped it open to page two. "It's clearly just an excuse for him to hang out with cool kids. Also, is that Olivia's coat, or is she wearing a llama?"

Clara had to smile. Maeve had some serious best-friend skills.

"Can't you talk to Wesley about it? Maybe change her mind?" Maeve stuffed the paper back in her bag.

Clara shook her head. She wasn't sure anyone was capable of changing Wesley's mind. Not even Mrs. Major, apparently.

They continued on, past the antique shop and the vintage clothing shop and the cheese shop, which today had only 12 TYPES OF GOUDA! but also 17 TYPES OF BRIE! As they passed the pasta shop blaring Sinatra, Maeve launched into another tap dance.

"Look, Clara, I know this seems awful," she said, snapping her fingers. "But this is just the beginning of your career in journalism. Here's what's going to happen: you're going to prove your chips—"

"Chops."

"—by writing the best horoscopes Wesley has ever seen. Then she'll have to give you a better assignment!" Maeve finished her dance with a flourish of jazz hands. "You will become a famous and successful investigative journalist. And I will be a famous and successful stage actress. And we'll travel the world together, performing and writing. Won't that be amazing?" She linked her arm in Clara's as they walked on. "We'll go to West Palm Beach to see Elaine, and then Hong Kong to see my grandparents. And then maybe Paris. Or Greece? I've always wanted to go to Greece."

Clara knew very little about Greece, but she liked the sound of the plan.

"And we'll have houses in the city too," Maeve bubbled on. "Side by side, of course, and close enough to my parents' place that we can zip over when my dad makes pizza. Hey, my dad's making pizza tonight! Want to come?"

Clara considered it; Mr. Healy-Lin made the best pizza she'd ever tasted. But she and her mother had plans to eat their combined weight in guacamole at Paquito's. She told Maeve as much. "Another time, though?" she said, stopping in front of Healing Herbs.

"Okay," Maeve agreed. "See you tomorrow, then, to rehearse? Let's meet in the park at eleven."

"The park?" Clara frowned. "I thought we'd go to your place."

Maeve shook her head. "My mom's having friends over for brunch. And I need to project." She tapped her chest.

"All right," Clara said, though she'd been looking forward to escaping the Market and going to Maeve's. "But if it rains . . . ?"

"It won't," said Maeve. "But I'll text you."

"Okay." Clara patted the cell phone in her pocket—an old one of Elaine's that her grandmother had left when she moved away.

"Because no one should live in Kensington Market without some way to call for help in case of emergency," Elaine had explained.

"Oh, Mom." Gaby had rolled her eyes. "There are people around all the time. Clara can just use her voice to call for help."

Clara wasn't sure how that conversation had ended; she'd pocketed the phone and slipped away.

"Enjoy the tacos," Maeve said, waving goodbye.

"I will," Clara promised. It was perhaps the only thing she enjoyed about her new neighborhood. Aside from Maeve, of course.

She turned and ran up the steps to Healing Herbs.

☙

"Cee!" Gaby cried as she stepped through the door. "I'm so glad you're here!"

"Me too," Clara sighed, shutting the door and checking the clock. It was nearly four o'clock; in one hour, she could flip the sign on the door to SORRY! WE'RE CLOSED! Flipping that sign was highly satisfying.

"Um, where are you?" she asked, looking around the empty shop.

"In the storeroom!" her mother called. "I'm showing some friends around!"

"Friends?" Clara's stomach sank.

Gaby strode out of the storeroom. She was wearing her favorite cotton skirt—the blue one with the constellation print—and she'd wrapped a matching blue scarf around her head. "Hi, darling!"

"This place is amazing, Gabs," someone said. A moment later, Gaby's new friend Lily stepped out of the storeroom, once again wearing her long black lace dress and the gloves that reached all the way up to her elbows. Perched on her head amongst her curls was what appeared to be a bird's nest.

"You do such incredible work!" someone else said, and a

man Clara had never seen before emerged from the store-room. He was easily six and a half feet tall, and dressed in wrinkled trousers and a suit jacket that looked like it had been snacked on by insects, or maybe rats. He reminded Clara of a character from one of Maeve's favorite movies, about a man who had scissors for hands. She'd spent a good part of that film hiding in the bathroom.

Her stomach pitched.

"Cee, meet Lily and Terence," said Gaby. "Guys, this is my daughter, Clara."

"Clara!" Lily cried. "It's *so* good to see you again!" She leaped over and took Clara's hands in hers.

"Pleased to meet you, Clara." Terence peered at Clara over Lily's shoulder. He had dark circles around his eyes, not unlike the man with the scissor-hands.

Clara fought the urge to run back outside. "Um, hi," she said, extracting her hands. "Nice, uh, necklace," she added politely, gesturing to the giant silver half-moon hanging from Terence's neck. There was actually nothing nice about it, but it was definitely hard to ignore.

Terence grinned. "Thanks! It's my newest creation. I dabble in jewelry making. Unique pieces for modern, mystical men."

"Terence is so creative," Lily cooed. "His company is called TalisMan. Get it? Because a talisman is like a magic charm, and these pieces are specifically for men."

"Got it." Clara took a step back. She could only imagine what Elaine would say about these two. "So, um, that's what you do for work? Make jewelry?"

Terence laughed. "Oh no, it's just a side project. Lily and I both work in real estate."

"Oh." Clara relaxed a bit. At least selling houses was a normal profession.

"And tell her what you *specialize* in," Gaby prompted.

Lily wiggled her eyebrows. "Haunted houses."

"Haunted . . . houses," Clara repeated.

Lily nodded. "Terence communes with the dead. He can walk into any house and know exactly how many ghosts live there. Condos too. You wouldn't think they'd be haunted, but they usually are." She squeezed Terence's arm. "You're so talented, sweet pea."

"But Lily is the brains of the operation," Terence said, petting the nest on her head.

Clara gave her mother an "is this for real?" look, but Gaby was busy arranging her herbs on the wall. She wondered if it was too late to run after Maeve and take her up on the pizza offer.

"I'm going to close up early today," Gaby said. "That way, we can get to Paquito's before the rest of the city does. It's really popular," she told her new friends. "And on Friday nights, it's always packed."

Clara doubted the owner of Healing Herbs would consider this a good reason to close up early, but she didn't argue. The sooner she could get away from her mother's new friends, the better. She went to flip the sign on the door.

"Oh, we know," said Lily. "Terence and I love Paquito's. Don't we, sweet pea?"

"Sure do," said Terence. "Thanks for inviting us."

"Wait, *you're* coming?" Clara turned back around.

"Didn't I mention that?" said Gaby. "Sorry, I'm so forgetful lately. Mercury in retrograde, you know."

"Oh *totally*," Lily and Terence chorused.

Clara flipped the sign with a smack.

Ten minutes later, they were all squished in a booth near Paquito's kitchen, far from Clara and Gaby's usual table for two by the window. Clara shifted on the sticky plastic seat and grimaced. This was *not* her idea of a fun Friday night.

"Chips and guac to start?" Paquito called as he hurried by on his way to the kitchen. Gaby gave him a thumbs-up and then leaned over to Clara. "I think he looks perkier, don't you? My philter must have done the trick."

Clara watched the chef zip around the kitchen, hauling vats of salsa and sour cream. She shrugged. "Maybe he just drank a bunch of coffee."

"Paquito's an insomniac," Gaby explained to her friends. "I made him an herbal philter to help him sleep."

"You're a miracle worker, Gabs!" Lily proclaimed.

"Like a modern apothecary," Terence added. "Or a witch."

Clara flinched on her mother's behalf. "No, she isn't—" she began, just as Gaby exclaimed, "Oh, thank you, Terence! That means so much."

Clara turned to her mother with an incredulous look. Sometimes she wondered how they were even related.

Fortunately, a waiter arrived to take their taco order and plunk down a bowl of chips and a giant bowl of guacamole. After he left, Lily turned to Gaby.

"It's not too personal to ask about Clara's dad, is it?"

If Clara's mouth hadn't been full of guac, she would have informed Lily that it absolutely *was* too personal. If Elaine had been there, she would have tossed Lily out of the restaurant for being so rude. Clara's dad was one of the things they tried never to talk about in Elaine's house.

There were a lot of those things, actually.

But Gaby only shrugged. "Bruce lives in Boston these days, but he's never been a part of our lives," she said. "He and I were only together for a little while, and we were so young, you know? Too young to know what we really needed." She munched on a chip. "We just weren't right for each other. He's a lawyer," she added.

"Ohhh," Terence and Lily nodded, as if this explained everything.

And, Clara had to admit, it actually did. She'd never met Bruce and had only ever seen one photo of him. In it, he was leaning casually on a golf club, beaming like he'd just hit a hole in one. He wore brilliant white shoes, a beige polo shirt and a taupe-colored sweater knotted around his neck. That told Clara all she needed to know: Bruce definitely wasn't her mother's kind of person.

He was, however, Elaine's kind of person. Every now and then, despite everyone's best efforts not to mention him, Bruce's name would pop up, and Elaine would sigh, "He was just so *down to earth*!"

"Mom, he was boring," Gaby would tell her.

"He was gainfully employed!" Elaine would point out. And Gaby would pretend to snore.

At this point, Clara liked to leave the room.

"Hey, Cee, how was your meeting today?" Gaby turned to her.

It took Clara a moment to remember her lunchtime *Gazette* meeting. It felt like ages ago. "Fine," she said, not wanting to discuss it.

Gaby put an arm around her shoulders. "My daughter is a budding journalist," she told her friends.

"Ooh la la!" said Lily.

"It's just a school newspaper." Clara focused on the guac, hoping they'd change the subject.

"That's cool," said Terence. "So what do you write?"

"She wrote an excellent profile of the school sewing club!" said Gaby.

"Knitting," Clara growled. "And I have a new assignment now."

As soon as the words left her mouth, she regretted them.

"Really? What is it?"

"Oh. Um. It's . . ." Clara picked up a chip and dipped it in guac. "The horoscopes," she mumbled.

All three adults gasped.

"That's the BEST part of the whole paper!" Lily squealed.

"No." Clara shoved the chip in her mouth. "It isn't."

"Oh, Cee, this is so exciting!" her mother cried. "You *know* how I feel about horoscopes."

"Uh-huh," said Clara. Which was precisely why she shouldn't have mentioned it.

"Do you know how to read the charts?" asked Terence.

Clara swallowed. "The what?"

"The charts," he said. "Astrology—that's the study of horoscopes—involves reading complex charts of planetary movement and alignment. I know a guy who's an expert. I could introduce you."

"Actually, Gabs, you should meet him," Lily added. "He might be your type. Right, sweet pea?" she said to Terence.

"Good call," said Terence. "He's a Sagittarius, like me. What's your sign, Gabs?"

"I'm a Gemini. With a rising moon in Taurus."

Lily gasped. "Oh, that explains so much!"

The server appeared with a platter of tacos just as Clara was about to bang her head on the table.

"Could I please get a coffee too?" Terence asked him. "I've got a long night ahead of me."

"Really? What's up for tonight?" asked Gaby. Clara noted a hint of envy in her voice, and it made her even more irritated. Friday nights at the Costas' usually involved eating popcorn and watching a not-scary movie on their laptop, which was just fine with Clara.

"A séance," Terence replied.

Clara threw her hands in the air. "Seriously?" Was there no end to these people's weirdness?

Terence nodded, picking up a taco. "It's another little side project of mine. On Friday nights, I host a séance at the Black

Cat Café on Queen Street. Some people bring requests—family or friends they'd like to contact in the afterworld."

"Terence has a real entrepreneurial spirit," Lily gushed.

Clara didn't even have the heart to point out the pun. She stuffed a taco in her mouth, even though her appetite was long gone. Then she pictured Maeve eating pizza with her parents, who had normal jobs that didn't involve communing with the dead. Next time, she told herself, she'd jump at the chance to spend Friday night with them, even if it involved watching scary crime shows on TV.

Because at least scary TV shows were just made up and could be avoided by hiding in the bathroom.

Real life wasn't so simple.

CHAPTER 7

"THIS HEAT!" MAEVE PRETENDED to swoon, collapsing beside Clara on the ground. After a moment's rest, she sat up. "Time for ice cream?"

"Time for ice cream!" Clara hopped up off the patch of grass where she'd been watching Maeve rehearse, and then pulled Maeve up with her. "Just let me stop in at the shop and ask my mom for money."

Maeve waved this away. "It's my treat. My dad gave me some." She patted her pocket; the coins inside jangled. "He knew we'd need sustenance after rehearsing."

Clara dusted off her jeans, eager to escape the park. If you could actually call it a park—she called it a poor excuse, at best.

"Look, Cee! We've got our own park!" That's what her mother had declared back in August, when they'd happened upon it while exploring their new neighborhood.

"That's a park?" Clara had said dubiously, taking in its few scrawny trees, ragged patches of grass and weathered playground equipment. She thought longingly of High Park, where she and Elaine would go for brisk walks three times a week at least. High Park had hundreds of towering trees and adorably fat chipmunks that begged for food, and even a pond for skating in winter. Clara particularly loved it in autumn, when the leaves turned red and gold, and she and Elaine and sometimes even Gaby would wander along the trails, boots crunching on fallen leaves. And Gaby would bring peanuts to feed the adorably fat chipmunks, and Elaine would lecture her about all the diseases they carried.

Clara sighed. She missed High Park. And it had been weeks now since she'd talked to Elaine.

They headed for Sophie's ice cream shop, which stood across the street from Paquito's. Clara peeled off her jacket and tied it around her waist as they walked. It was unseasonably warm for October, especially in the Market, which had few trees to cool it down. Though it was just after noon, the streets teemed with people shopping for groceries, eating brunch on patios, and trying on sunglasses and fedoras at little sidewalk kiosks.

Clara had to admit her mother had been right about the cell phone: if she ever needed to call for help, a few hundred people would always be around to hear her.

"You know?" said Maeve. "It's just so frustrating."

"Sorry, what?" Clara tuned back in, sidestepping a trio of Chihuahuas tied to a post. They were only slightly larger than the rats Clara sometimes spotted in the alley behind Healing Herbs.

"My audition." Maeve crouched to pat the dogs. "I think I could nail it if it weren't for the fact that Morris Mumford is a man. I mean, don't get me wrong, I can play a man. But Ms. Flynn will probably give the role to Jin—you know, the dinosaur guy? And he's a decent actor, but he doesn't have . . ." —she stood up and tossed an imaginary detective's hat in the air— "panache!"

It was an excellent word; Clara filed it away for future use. "Maybe Ms. Flynn could change the script and make Morris Mumford a . . . Moira," she suggested as she pulled open the door to Sophie's ice cream parlor and stepped inside. "Ah, sweet air-conditioning."

"Glorious," Maeve agreed. "This was an excellent idea, if I do say so myself."

Unfortunately, a few dozen other people had had the same one; the lineup for ice cream stretched all the way to the door. Sophie and her two assistants were scooping like mad behind the counter.

"Moira Mumford," Maeve mused as they joined the queue. "Or maybe Molly? Either way, I like the idea. It would mean I wouldn't have to wear a fake mustache." She twitched her upper lip. "Plus, women can solve crimes every bit as well as men, right?"

Clara agreed.

"Like you. You could have solved the Buzzter mystery just as well as Preston. Probably a hundred times better, actually."

Clara swallowed. She'd been trying to forget about the Buzzter incident.

"Sorry," Maeve said quickly.

Clara shrugged. "Whatever. It's just a missing mascot.

It's not a story that matters anyway." At least, that's what she'd been telling herself.

"Sure it matters. He's our school mas—" Maeve began, but she stopped herself when Clara gave her an exasperated look. "Right. Anyway, the question is, should I audition as a woman detective, or should I suck it up and be a man?"

Clara agreed that it was a quandary. "You're going to nail it, whatever you do," she told Maeve. She just had a feeling.

"What is the hold up?" a man in front of them grumbled. "This is taking forever!"

Clara stood on tiptoe to see what was causing it. "Hey, that's Paquito!"

He stood at the front counter, where he seemed to be trying to decide between ice cream flavors. Sophie stood across from him, smiling patiently.

"Make up your mind, buddy," the man in front of them muttered.

"We'd better decide what we want now," said Maeve. "Chocolate Birthday Cake? Or Chocolate Caramel Swirl? Ooh, maybe Death by Chocolate—that sounds like it's to die for!" She laughed. "Get it?"

But Clara was watching Paquito as he shifted from one foot to the other, lifting his Jays cap and setting it back down again. Was his insomnia slowing him down? she wondered. She made a mental note to tell her mother to make him a stronger remedy. Or maybe he needed something else altogether.

When their turn finally came, Maeve and Clara made their orders (Chocolate Birthday Cake and Strawberry 'n'

Sprinkles, respectively) and carried their cones over to a table by the window.

"This feels very grown-up," Maeve observed, and Clara agreed. When she and Gaby lived with Elaine, she hadn't been allowed to wander around the neighborhood by herself. She could only imagine what her grandmother would say if she saw Clara and Maeve dining solo in the Market.

As much as she missed Elaine, she had to admit it was nice to have some freedom.

"Speaking of grown-up, my dad was helping me map out our voyage last night," Maeve said.

"Our what?"

"Our voyage," Maeve repeated. "You know. The big trip we'll take when we're old enough to travel by ourselves. West Palm Beach, Hong Kong, Greece . . . Hey, where does the rest of your family live? We should go visit them too."

"Oh." Clara shrugged. "We're a small family."

It wasn't a lie, exactly. Her immediate family consisted of Gaby and Elaine. She'd never known her grandfather, who'd passed away when Gaby was little.

There were others, though—at least a few, out there somewhere. But her family was another thing Elaine didn't like to talk about. Clara had asked Gaby about it once, years ago, and Gaby had told her what she knew: Elaine had a few cousins in Vancouver, maybe an aunt in the UK. But she'd lost touch with them all.

"They're not her people," Gaby had explained. So Clara

let it go, though she'd always thought it would be nice to have a few more family members.

She tuned back in to Maeve's monologue; apparently now they were going to London too, to visit the theater where Mrs. Healy-Lin had recited her first lines onstage, as a company member in *My Fair Lady*. And then on to Paris and Madrid and—

"Oh my gosh. Clara, look!" Maeve spun toward the window, nearly smearing it with chocolate ice cream. "That *car*!"

Clara squinted at the little gray hatchback rattling by outside the ice cream shop. It halted with a wheeze and a clunk. On its side, someone had painted the words "Home Sweet Haunted Home: A real estate company that's out of this world!" in big red script.

"Oh," Clara breathed. "Oh *no*."

The car doors swung open, and out hopped Lily and Terence.

"Clara!" Maeve squealed. "It's that woman from the shop! Lily, remember?"

Clara nodded. She hadn't told Maeve about the previous night's dinner, not wanting to relive the horror. She desperately hoped they weren't in the mood for ice cream.

Fortunately, her mother's new friends seemed to have other business to attend to, and they hurried off down the street.

Maeve laughed. "They're amazing. Clara, Kensington Market has the coolest people in the whole city. How can you not want to live here forever?"

Clara raised an eyebrow at her and then turned back to her ice cream cone. She didn't even know where to begin.

✦

"I'll be upstairs," she told her mother later that afternoon as she breezed through Healing Herbs. Gaby was concocting a remedy for a man in a motorcycle jacket, who was telling her about his plantar warts in great detail. Clara ducked into the storeroom and then took the stairs two at a time up to the dark hallway. Gaby had recently visited her favorite paint shop on College Street and returned home with an armload of paint chips in every hue imaginable. She'd taped them to the hallway walls in attempts to decide which color to paint them. Clara passed a Dijon Mustard Yellow, a Sugarplum Rose and a Tropical Seaweed Green. She couldn't decide which was worse.

She let herself into the apartment and paused for a moment, relishing the feeling of being alone. Music and laughter from the street below drifted in through the open windows—there was really no escaping it in the Market. But at least she had the apartment all to herself.

She pulled out her phone and scrolled through her short list of contacts. After the previous night's dinner with her mother's new friends, she needed a good dose of her grandmother more than ever.

She clicked on the photo beside Elaine's name. Clara herself had snapped it shortly before they'd all moved out of the duplex. In it, Elaine was sitting on her taupe-colored couch, drinking a cup of black coffee. Her short gray hair was neatly curled, and she stared at the camera without smiling. Elaine had never really been one for smiling.

She texted her grandmother: Are you free to talk?

The answer came promptly. Elaine was nothing if not prompt.

I'm out for the afternoon, dear. Another day?

"Shoot," Clara muttered. So much for her afternoon plans. Now she'd have to do homework or—

"Horoscopes," she groaned, recalling her looming deadline. It was the last thing she wanted to do on a Saturday afternoon.

And yet, she realized, it wasn't a bad idea to write them while her mother was at work. If Gaby saw her composing horoscopes, she'd insist on helping, which would likely involve reading about every astrological sign and discussing them in great detail.

Clara had no time or patience for that.

"Fine then." She stood up and searched the living room bookshelf for Gaby's massive *Guide to the Zodiac*, which she'd bought at the used bookstore the same day she'd found *Herbal Alchemy*. It smelled like dust and mold, and Clara held it by the spine and gave it a good shake, just to make sure there weren't any bedbugs hiding in the pages. Elaine once told her that bedbugs could hide in library and secondhand books—as well as in movie theaters and on subway seats. Clara hadn't sat down on a subway since then.

She hauled the book and the laptop back to her bedroom and began her assignment.

According to the chapter titled "Introduction to the Zodiac," there were twelve astrological signs, each one connected with a thirty-degree arc of sky above the earth. As the earth moves around the sun, it explained, the sun appears to pass from one of these arcs to the next; in one year, it passes through them all. So someone whose birthday falls between June 21 and July 22, like Clara, was born when the sun was in the zodiac sign of Cancer. Cancer, in other words, was her "sun sign."

That much Clara could understand, but then the introduction went on to say that all the people born under the same sun sign possessed many similar characteristics. Cancers, for example, tended to be kind, compassionate and a little moody.

"I am not moody," Clara huffed. And the idea was ridiculous: how could everyone born within a month of each other have the same characteristics, or similar futures? That didn't make sense at all.

She decided to skip the "Introduction to the Zodiac."

The rest of the book was divided into twelve chapters, one for each sun sign. Each chapter described the personalities and preferences of people born under that sign, as well as how they got along with the other signs.

"Woo," Clara muttered. But she flipped to the Gemini chapter, just for interest's sake.

Geminis are friendly, upbeat and spontaneous creatures with infectious smiles, the book said. *They can adapt to most any situation, and they attract friends from far and wide. One thing is for sure: life with a Gemini is never boring!*

It was, Clara had to admit, a fitting description of both her mother and her best friend. But could it possibly be true for everyone born between May 21 and June 20? Not likely.

She flipped on to the Virgo chapter. Virgos were born between August 23 and September 22, and as Gaby had pointed out time and again, Elaine was a "textbook Virgo."

Virgos are nothing if not useful. They live to help others, in a down-to-earth and practical way. Always prompt and detail-oriented, a Virgo can whip even the most chaotic situation into order. Many strive for perfection in everything they do.

"Hmm." Clara frowned. It was pretty well the perfect description of Elaine. But that was just a coincidence, wasn't it? There had to be millions of Virgos who were nothing like her grandmother.

She sighed. Already this task was taking too long. She'd have to hustle if she wanted to finish before Gaby closed up shop.

She opened a new document on the laptop and began to compose a horoscope for Virgo, with her grandmother in mind.

She pictured Elaine in her new apartment at the senior's complex, eating her dry toast alone at her kitchen table, listening to the palm trees rustling outside her open window, and maybe reading the West Palm Beach newspaper. Was she lonely? she wondered. Did she sometimes miss Gaby and Clara?

You've gone through some big changes lately, Virgo, Clara wrote. *And you might be feeling a bit unsettled. Joining a class or learning a new skill could help you meet new people and find your groove.*

She read over the fortune, and it made her smile. Elaine had never been one for learning new skills, and Clara couldn't imagine that changing in West Palm Beach.

Still, it was a fine horoscope, so she moved on, flipping back to the previous chapter in the *Guide to the Zodiac*: Leo.

Leos, born between July 23 and August 22, are warmhearted and likable, creative and generous. Some seek the spotlight, while others prefer to lead and inspire quietly.

Do I know any Leos? Clara wondered. Then she snapped her fingers. "Paquito!" On the very first night she and Gaby had dined at his restaurant, back in August, one of the servers had pulled Paquito out of the kitchen and fastened a sparkly birthday hat to his bald head. Then she'd forced Paquito to stand in the middle of the restaurant while everyone sang him "Happy Birthday," to his great embarrassment.

Clara pictured him in line at Sophie's ice cream shop earlier that day, hemming and hawing over his order. Then she wrote:

Try to be a bit more assertive this month, Leo. If there's something on your mind, come out and say it. Be bold and decisive, like the lion you are!

She paused to reread the fortune, and liked the sound of it. It sounded right. She pushed on.

Pretty soon, she'd established a system: if she didn't know

anyone with a particular sun sign, she'd make up a fortune that could apply to almost anyone. The Scorpios of KMS, for instance, would soon be embarking on a journey. The Capricorns had better study hard for an upcoming test—it wouldn't be nearly as simple as they thought.

But if she knew someone with the sign, she'd write a fortune specifically for that person. Maeve the Gemini, for example, could expect exciting career success in her future. Clara even wrote one for Terence, who'd mentioned that he was a Sagittarius. Recalling the rattling hatchback he and Lily had driven through the Market earlier, she wrote: *Transportation troubles await, Sagittarius. Now is not the time to put off fixing your ride. And while you're at it, why not consider a haircut?*

An hour later, she had twelve complete horoscopes. She edited each one carefully, since Wesley had zero tolerance for grammar errors. Then she wrote a quick email to the editor-in-chief, attached the document and hit send, crossing her fingers that Wesley would like them.

But not too much, of course. Because Clara never wanted to get stuck writing horoscopes again.

CHAPTER 8

OVER THE NEXT WEEK, CLARA MANAGED

to put the horoscopes out of her mind and concentrate on more important things, like science reports and spelling quizzes and trying to talk her mother out of painting the hallway a color called Lemon Meringue. In fact, she pretty well forgot about them until the following Tuesday's *Gazette* meeting, when Wesley presented the late-October issue, hot off the presses.

"It's looking pretty good, Newsies," she said as she passed around crisp new copies. Clara slid over to share with Lina again. "The production team did a fine job on the design, and they worked over the weekend to finish it." She nodded to some kids at the far end of the table. "Well done, guys."

The production team nodded back, looking a little bleary-eyed.

Lina flipped straight to her comic on page three. "Ugh," she grunted. "It looks awful!"

"No, it doesn't." Clara peered over her shoulder. The strip told the story of a kid who decided he'd rather have a good hair day than wear a bike helmet on his ride to school. Unsurprisingly, it didn't end well; the last panel showed him carried off on a stretcher, his hair a mess of blood and gravel. Clara cringed at the sight. "You did a great job," she told Lina, looking away from the carnage.

Lina shook her head. "It's not nearly graphic enough to get the point across." She snapped the paper shut. "Three days isn't enough time to create a quality comic. This new publishing schedule is totally unfair."

"Guys, pay attention," Wesley snapped. "And don't wrinkle your paper."

"Sorry." Clara quickly smoothed out the paper. Lina only grunted.

Wesley directed everyone's attention to the front page, which once again featured an article by Ravi Kang.

Now *that's* unfair, Clara thought, but she had to admit he'd written a captivating headline: "Hot on the Trail of the Counterfeit Kid." Ravi hadn't managed to find out who was forging the sick notes, but he'd done an in-depth interview with Mr. James, the administrative assistant, who was taking a course in handwriting analysis, determined to track down the offender. Clara made a mental note to tell Mr. James about the Morris Mumford forgery episode next time she stopped by the office.

"Hang on," Sienna piped up. "What about the Buzzter story? Shouldn't that be front-page news?"

"Second page," said Wesley. Everyone flipped to page two.

At first glance, Clara could see exactly why Preston hadn't earned the front page. His headline read, "What Happened to Buzzter?", which was possibly the lamest headline she'd ever seen. She couldn't believe Wesley hadn't changed it.

But even worse than the headline was the article itself—or rather, the lack thereof. Instead of writing an investigative piece, Preston had taken a series of photos. The first showed the podium where Buzzter used to perch. It was empty except for his limp yellow necktie.

The second photo featured Mr. Devlin, seated at his desk wearing a Hawaiian-print shirt and looking grim. Then came a series of photos of kids posing with Buzzter's necktie: first the captain of the girls' basketball team; then Marcus Nilsson, who'd won the cooking contest for his cheese soufflé; and finally, once again, Olivia Silva. She was actually wearing the necktie, and she'd paired it with a yellow rain poncho.

"That's it?" Clara whispered. "Seriously?"

"Cool photos, Preston," said Lizzie.

"The one of Mr. Devlin is great," Ravi added.

Yeah, but where's the story? Clara wondered. Only when everyone turned her way did she realize she'd said it aloud.

"Oh. Um." She flushed, but she couldn't take it back. Wesley raised her eyebrows. "I mean, well," Clara stammered, "isn't it supposed to be investigative? This doesn't even tell us what happened to Buzzter or name any possible suspects."

"It's a photo essay," Preston sniffed, picking up his camera and fiddling with some buttons. "It's more a work of art than a story."

"But it's a newspaper!" Again the thought escaped Clara's mouth before she could stop it. She gulped and looked to Wesley for backup. Surely she wasn't satisfied with the photo essay. She couldn't be!

But Wesley only shrugged. "It is a departure for the *Gazette*," she admitted. "But we'll publish it and see what our readers think. Like I said, sometimes in journalism, you have to try new things, and then evaluate their success and adjust your strategy."

"Yeah." Preston glared at Clara.

Clara sank back in her chair. She was no journalism expert, but she was pretty certain they'd missed a big opportunity. It just didn't make sense.

But she stayed quiet as they flipped through the rest of the issue, past the volleyball game reports and the bike helmet comic strip, which everyone agreed was suitably graphic. They perused the classified ads and the cafeteria lunch specials and an update on the tuna casserole story (the cafeteria staff had agreed to change the name of the dish to Canned Haddock Casserole).

Finally, they came to the very last page, the new home for the KMS *Gazette* horoscopes, by Clara—

"Voyant?" Clara looked up at Wesley. "That's not my name."

Wesley beamed. "I know! Isn't it brilliant? I thought of it right before we went to print, so I told the production team to stop the presses! Remember, guys?" She looked at the kids at the far end of the table, who once again nodded, looking less than thrilled.

"It's your new *nom de plume*," Wesley went on. "Clara Voyant. Get it? Because you're a clairvoyant! That's someone who can see the future, you know."

"I know," Clara said, looking back down at the paper. Of course she knew that. She just didn't want to *be* that.

"That's a perfect name!" Lizzie cried, and a few other Newsies nodded.

"I know, right?" Wesley looked very pleased with herself. "Our readers are going to love it. And that's why I've decided to keep you on horoscopes all year, Clara."

Clara's mouth fell open.

"I know," Wesley went on. "It's a big deal. Not every Newbie Newsy gets their own column, although I did too, back in sixth grade. But I think this is a good fit. So congratulations, Clara Voyant!"

Ravi and Lina started to applaud. Clara struggled to close her mouth. An entire *year* of horoscopes?

"Hey!" Lizzie jabbed the paper with a finger. "Look at this! I'm a Taurus, and my horoscope says I'll find something I lost." She looked up at Clara. "And that's true—I found my favorite ring two days ago. I hadn't seen it in a year!" She held up her right hand; a gold band glinted on her ring finger. "How did you do that?"

Clara shrugged, still trying to process Wesley's announcement. "I just made it up." She hadn't known a single Taurus, so she'd pulled that fortune out of the air.

"Well, it's pretty incredible." Lizzie looked from Clara to her ring, and then back to Clara.

Wesley frowned at Lizzie. "You don't really believe in horoscopes, do you?"

Lizzie held up her hand again, as if that explained everything.

"Right." Wesley rolled her eyes. "Okay, Newsies, back to business. Fold up those newspapers *neatly* and hand them back to me. Come on." She clapped her hands. "We've got a lot more to discuss today."

Clara folded up her newspaper and handed it back, still trying to understand what had just happened. A horoscope column. By Clara Voyant. Hers for *the rest of the year*.

This was definitely not part of the plan.

In fact, it had disaster written all over it.

CHAPTER 9

AFTER THE *GAZETTE* MEETING, Clara gathered her things and headed for the auditorium, where the auditions for *The Seventh Slipper: A Morris Mumford Mystery* were in full swing. She hoped Maeve's turn would be over, so they could walk home together and commiserate about Preston's awful photo essay and Clara's tragic fate.

But a sign on the auditorium door read: AUDITIONS IN PROGRESS. PLEASE BE QUIET!

Clara sighed. Apparently she'd be walking home by herself. She headed for her locker to get her backpack.

On the way, she passed the gymnasium where, judging by the cheers and stomps and sneaker squeaks she could hear, a game was in progress. In no hurry to head out into a drizzly afternoon, she slipped inside to watch for a minute or two.

It was a boys' basketball game, and the Hornets were trailing, 36 to 12. The opposing team, the Pirates, were sinking one shot after another, barely breaking a sweat while the Hornets stumbled and fumbled, as if they'd just rolled out of bed.

"Pirates Pummel Haggard Hornets"—that's what Clara's headline would read, if she were the *Gazette* sports reporter assigned to cover the game. Then she looked around the gym to see if Matt and Sienna were witnessing it. She couldn't see either one, but she did spot Mr. Devlin, standing just a few feet away with Ms. Thien, the science teacher, Mr. James, the administrative assistant, and—

Mrs. Major, the custodian. Clara's heart stuttered at the sight of her.

She stood beside Mr. Devlin, arms folded over her chest, looking like she wanted to charge out onto the court and pummel the Pirates right back.

Clara was about to leave when she heard Ms. Thien say, "It's just a coincidence, Jim."

Mr. Devlin sighed. "I don't know, Anna. This has been happening ever since Buzzter went missing." He stared out at the court, shaking his head.

"It's only been five days," Ms. Thien pointed out.

"In which time we've lost seven games!" said Mr. Devlin. "Basketball, volleyball, badminton—you name it, we got massacred at it."

Clara made a mental note to pass this information on to Sienna and Matt. Obviously it was a coincidence, but it could still make a good story.

Suddenly, Mrs. Major turned on her heel and headed for the door. Clara stepped hurriedly out of her path.

But just as Mrs. Major was marching by, she stopped abruptly. Clara's heart stopped with her.

Mrs. Major looked down at Clara's feet, and then up at her face. Her gray eyes narrowed. "Outdoor shoes?"

"In-in-indoor!" Clara squeaked.

Mrs. Major nodded. Then she marched out of the gym.

Clara waited until her heart resumed beating and her legs no longer felt like overcooked noodles. Then she bolted for the door. She was completely, utterly done with school for the day.

Outside, it was starting to spit. Clara pulled up her hood and shoved her hands in her pockets.

Horoscopes all year long, she thought as she trudged toward the Market. She did a few calculations. That was *sixteen* rounds of horoscopes! *One hundred and ninety-two* fortunes! How could she possibly survive it? And would Wesley never let her write anything else?

She recalled Preston's photo essay and groaned aloud. She still couldn't believe Wesley had let him get away with it.

By the time she reached Healing Herbs, the drizzle had turned to steady rain. She stormed up the steps, pushed open the door and nearly collided with her mother.

"Cee, you're right on time! Don't take off your coat," Gaby told her.

"Why not?" Clara snapped. Then she noticed that her mother was wearing her long purple trench coat. "What's going on?"

"We're going out," said Gaby. "I'm closing up early."

"Again?" Clara didn't like the sound of this.

Gaby flipped the sign on the door. "Terence and Lily invited us over for tea!"

"Oh no," Clara said. There was absolutely *no way*. "No. I'll stay home."

"Cee! I told them we'd both come. It'll be fun, I promise."

Clara didn't believe that for a second. "Mom," she said, trying to keep her cool, "I really don't want to. I have a lot of homework to do."

"We won't be long," Gaby assured her. "You need a break after school—you work so much." She pushed back Clara's hood and smoothed her hair. "And anyway, this is about making new friends and building community. We need that, both of us."

"I don't need that," Clara grumped.

But Gaby was pulling her out the door, back into the rain. "Lily's going to read our tea leaves! Isn't that cool? She'll tell us our fortunes."

Clara groaned again. Could this day get any worse? "Mom, seriously—"

"We'll be back in an hour," Gaby promised, squeezing her hand. She pulled Clara down the block, past Sophie's ice cream shop, a jewelry store and two cafés, and then down some steps to a basement-level door. A sign on the door read HOME SWEET HAUNTED HOME!

Clara felt ill.

Gaby knocked, and a moment later, Lily flung open the door. "Sweet peas! You're here!" She dragged them inside. "Come see our office headquarters—this is where the magic happens."

Unsurprisingly, Home Sweet Haunted Home headquarters looked like no office Clara had ever seen. The walls were red like the Costas' kitchen, but darker and creepier: more of a Blood Bath than a Ripe Tomato. Two black desks stood side by side on one end of the room; a black table, black chairs and a black leather couch stood on the other. Candles flickered on the desks and table.

Of course they light their office with candles, Clara thought. Of course they do. She tried to give her mother a "this had better only take an hour" look, but it was hard to make her out in the candlelight.

"Hi, guys!" Terence walked over, a cell phone pressed to his ear. "I'll just be a second," he whispered, pointing at the phone. "Oh, totally," he said into it. "That attic is haunted for sure—I sensed one spirit right away, and there could be one more. But I'm not getting bad vibes. I expect she went in peace and is now watching over the place. But I'll tell you what: I'll go back on Saturday and chat her up, get the deets on her passing and how things are going in the afterlife. What do you say?"

Clara and Gaby turned to Lily, who grinned and held up two crossed fingers. "We've got a big sale on the line."

Clara took a breath and imagined what Elaine would do if she knew Gaby had dragged Clara for tea at the Home Sweet Haunted Home headquarters. She'd probably hop the first plane back to Toronto to put a stop to the madness. Imagining it made Clara feel a bit better.

Of course, the problem with Elaine swooping in to save the day would be that she'd witness, in real life, how Clara and Gaby lived now. She'd have to sit on a wobbly kitchen chair and listen to the squirrels tap-dancing on the roof and get tangled in the beaded curtain every time she entered the apartment.

Clara cringed at the thought. As much as she wanted to see her grandmother, she didn't want that.

Terence finished his phone call, and they all sat down on black chairs at the black table for tea in white mugs.

"I know they don't match the color scheme." Lily giggled as she passed them around. "But I need to see the leaves at the bottom."

Clara stared at the tea leaves swirling in her mug, and one of Elaine's favorite phrases popped to mind: "Sometimes, the only way out is through." She often said that when faced with a disagreeable task, like shoveling the walk after a snowstorm or having dinner with the neighbors.

The only way out is through, Clara told herself, picking up her mug. The sooner she drank up, the sooner she could leave.

She guzzled her mug of tea. It tasted like grass clippings, with a hint of mushrooms.

"Nice work, Clara!" Lily grabbed for her mug. "You just couldn't wait to have your fortune told, could you?"

"Something like that," Clara mumbled, wiping her mouth.

"I'm happy to oblige," Lily said, tucking her legs up under her on the chair. "Do you know much about tasseography?"

"About what?" Clara and Gaby said in unison.

"Jinx!" Gaby chirped. Clara gave her a tired look. She was in no mood for games.

"Tasseography is the study of patterns in tea leaves," Terence said, slurping his tea. "And coffee grounds and wine stains too."

"It's quite a science," Lily said, peering into Clara's mug.

Clara shook her head. What was with these people and their fake sciences?

"Ooh, how long have you been studying, Lil?" asked Gaby.

"Since I was about Clara's age. Actually . . ." Lily stood up from the table, crossed the room to a black bookshelf and returned with a book. "My mother gave me this when I first began my studies. I've been thinking of passing it on to you since we met, Clara." She held it out.

"Me?" Clara said, eyeing the faded paperback. "Oh. Um. You don't have to do that."

"No, really, I want you to have it." Lily sat down and picked up Clara's mug again. "I have a strong feeling that you'd make an excellent tea-leaf reader."

"Yes!" cried Gaby, just as Clara said, "Oh no."

Her mother gave her a wide-eyed look, so Clara added, "No, thank you."

Lily shrugged. "Well, let's see what your leaves say about it." She squinted into Clara's mug. "Hmm. Wow."

"What?" Gaby leaned forward. "What do you see?"

"It's an eagle," said Lily.

"Ooh," Gaby breathed.

"Mom, you don't even know what that means," said Clara.

"Well, it sounds majestic," said Gaby.

Clara took another deep breath. "You actually see an

eagle in there?" she asked Lily, who nodded and passed her the mug. Clara peered inside. All she saw was a clump of leaves. She passed it back.

"It takes time," Terence assured her. "Don't worry. It'll come with practice."

"I'm not worried," Clara informed him.

Her mother nudged her foot under the table. "Tell us what the eagle means, Lily."

"It normally represents ambition, drive and mastery of skills," said Lily. "But I'm sensing something else." She looked at Clara for a long moment. "Something like . . . fame?"

"Fame?" said Clara and Gaby.

"Would you stop that?" Clara hissed.

Lily nodded, still staring at Clara. "I think you're going to be famous, Clara. And in the very near future."

Clara shivered, wishing Lily would stop looking at her so intently. It was creeping her out. "I don't think so," she said.

"It's probably for your journalism," said Gaby. "Right, Lil?"

Lily looked at the so-called eagle in the mug again. Then she looked back up at Clara. "Hmm. I don't know . . ."

Suddenly, Clara wanted very much to go home. Had an hour passed yet? She searched for a clock but couldn't find one.

"Oh hey, Gabs." Terence set his mug down on the table. "We have to postpone our trip to Mystic Mart."

"Oh no. Really?"

"To where?" Clara asked, wondering how often her mother now made plans with these people.

"Mystic Mart," said Terence. "You should come, Clara. It sells every supernatural supply you could imagine: tarot cards, tea leaves, potion recipe books . . . I get my jewelry supplies there too."

"And it's enormous," Lily added. "Think Walmart, but with voodoo dolls."

"I can't wait!" said Gaby.

Clara vowed to be sick that day.

"Anyway, we'll have to wait a few days," said Terence. "Our car broke down last night. Muffler issues." He passed his mug to Lily, who peered inside.

Clara recalled their hatchback rattling down Kensington Avenue and pulling up outside Sophie's. Of course it had broken down. Hadn't she—

Predicted it.

She'd predicted it in Terence's horoscope.

Lily glanced up from Terence's mug and gave her a curious look. "You okay there, Clara?"

Clara nodded. It was just a coincidence. Obviously. She picked up the tasseography book and pretended to leaf through it until Lily eventually turned back to Terence's mug.

"Ooh, sweet pea!" she cried. "This looks like a cabbage if I've ever seen one! There's money in your future!"

Terence and Gaby cheered. Clara kept her head down, pretending to be engrossed in a book she would never read willingly, and waiting for it all to be over.

CHAPTER 10

"MEETING ADJOURNED, NEWSIES!"

Wesley Ferris snapped her laptop shut as the clock struck one that Friday afternoon. "Remember, your articles are due on Monday morning this time. I want them in my inbox by 9 a.m. sharp."

"This is ridiculous," Lina grumbled to Clara as she packed up her sketchbook. "I've only drawn two panels of my comic so far. And look!" She held up her hand.

"Look at what?" asked Clara.

"My wrist! It's all swollen from drawing so fast," Lina said, flexing her wrist.

Clara hummed sympathetically, but she didn't ask questions. She needed Lina—and all the other Newsies—to leave the classroom so she could talk to Wesley alone.

She pretended to rearrange the books in her backpack until everyone had left. When the coast was finally clear, she rallied her courage and made her request.

"You want *another* assignment?" Wesley's shoulder pads crept up toward her ears. "But Clara, I gave you your own column! I don't just hand those things out, you know."

"I know. And I'm grateful," Clara lied. "But I have a good idea for an article—a follow-up to Preston's piece. Not that his photo essay wasn't good," she added hastily. "It was, you know, photographic. But there's more to the Buzzter story than what his photos told, and I could investigate the rest of it. Have you heard about the Hornets losing all their games?"

Wesley raised an eyebrow.

"Since Buzzter went missing, they've lost every one," Clara said. "Basketball, volleyball, badminton—you name it, they got massacred at it. I mean, it's obviously just a coincidence, but it's still a story. An important one," she finished, praying that Wesley would agree. She *had* to.

"Hmm." Wesley frowned again. "Well, it's not a bad idea."

"Right?" Clara cried, relieved. "It'll be great, I—"

"But it's Preston's story," Wesley went on. "If you went and rewrote it, that would violate the Journalists' Code of Ethics."

"The what?" asked Clara.

"The Journalists' Code of Ethics," said Wesley. "I have a copy hanging above my bed, you know. I study it before I go to sleep every night. You should get one too if you're serious about journalism."

"Um, okay," said Clara, who hadn't even known the Journalists' Code of Ethics existed. "But look, I wouldn't be rewriting his story, because he didn't write a story to begin with. So how would this be breaking the Code?"

"It's kind of complicated." Wesley smiled at her as if she were a toddler: cute, but not very smart. "Look it up online, okay? So, have you finished your horoscopes already? They are due Monday, you know."

"I know," Clara replied, gritting her teeth. "I'm almost finished them. They take no time to write."

"Well, maybe you should spend more time on them," Wesley suggested, fastening the clasps on her briefcase. "You know, work on really *becoming* Clara Voyant."

Clara didn't trust herself to answer that. She nodded, tight-lipped, and left the classroom.

"Becoming Clara Voyant," she huffed as she wove through the crowded hallway. "I don't want to become Clara Voyant. I want to become a journalist!"

"Clara, look!" Maeve cried as Clara marched up to her locker, still muttering to herself. She waved a copy of the *Gazette*, which had landed on newsstands throughout the school that morning.

"You got a copy," Clara said flatly. It was the last thing she wanted to look at.

"I got three!" Maeve grinned. "Everyone will want to read your horoscopes."

Clara opened her locker. "I don't know about that."

"I do," Maeve insisted. "Also, I saw the fortune you wrote for Gemini! You're the best friend ever!"

"I am?" Clara tried to remember what she'd written.

Maeve flipped the paper over. "It's an exciting time for you, Gemini," she read. "Well-deserved career success lies ahead. Your star is rising!" Maeve looked up and beamed. "You wrote that on purpose, for my audition!"

Clara couldn't deny it.

"Wow." Maeve reread her fortune. "So if I end up getting my part, it'll prove that you're actually a clairvoyant!"

"Huh? No, it won't." Clara shook her head. "You're going to get your part because you're a great actress. That has nothing to do with me."

Maeve tucked her newspaper into her binder. "We'll see, Clara Voyant. We'll see. I should find out today if I got a second audition. Or maybe on Monday."

"You will," Clara told her, because of course she would. And her stomach pinched with envy. It wasn't very best-friend-y of her, but she couldn't help it. She wanted her own star to rise alongside Maeve's.

*

All Clara wanted that evening was to forget about the horoscopes and eat her weight in Paquito's guacamole in peace.

But it was not to be.

"Excuse me, sir." Gaby leaned over and tapped the table next to theirs. "What's your sign?"

"Mom! Stop it," Clara whispered.

"Me? Um, I'm a Taurus," the man beside them said over a mouthful of fajita.

"Uh-huh, I thought so." Gaby consulted the *Gazette* horoscopes. "You're going to find something you lost long ago. Isn't that great?"

"Um, sure." He forced a smile.

"My daughter wrote these horoscopes," Gaby added.

"Mom, you're killing me." Clara slouched down in her chair, wishing once again that she'd skipped out on Friday night at Paquito's.

"I'm just so proud of you!" Gaby beamed. "And I'm excited about my imminent career success," she added, pointing at the Gemini horoscope. "My star is rising, Cee!"

"I wrote that for—" Clara began, but her mother was waving down the taco chef.

"Paquito! You're a Leo, right?" she called as he hustled by with a vat of sour cream balanced on one shoulder. "According to a highly qualified clairvoyant, you should be more assertive this month. If there's something on your mind, come out and say it. Be bold and decisive, like the lion you are!"

Under his Jays cap, Paquito's cheeks turned Ripe Tomato red. Clara put her head in her hands.

As soon as she got home that night, she grabbed her phone and sent her grandmother a text. It was only 8 p.m. in Florida; surely she was still awake.

Can you talk tonight? It's been *FOREVER*!

Then she waited, tapping her toe on the cold floor. "Mom, can you kick the heater?" she called.

A moment later, she heard Gaby boot the radiator. It rattled and wheezed like Terence and Lily's hatchback.

The hatchback she'd predicted would need repairing.

"Stop it," she told herself.

The phone buzzed, and she snatched it up.

I can't chat tonight, dear. I'm off to salsa lessons. Maybe another day? XO

"*Salsa lessons?*" Clara nearly dropped the phone.

"What's that?" Gaby called.

"Elaine's taking salsa lessons!" she yelled.

"Is that a joke?" asked Gaby.

"Exactly," said Clara. She read the message three more times, wondering if maybe autocorrect had mangled it. Or perhaps Elaine was learning to *make* salsa. That made more sense. Dancing the salsa would involve strangers in her "personal space," and Elaine had zero tolerance for that.

She was about to text back for clarification when the phone buzzed again. This time, it was a message from Maeve.

Clara! I got it! I got a second audition!!!

Then came a series of emojis: fireworks, cupcakes, rainbows and a girl turning cartwheels.

Clara laughed. Of course you did! she messaged back. Congrats!

Then her stomach pinched again, and she set down the phone and swallowed hard. Be a good friend, she told herself.

Maeve texted back within seconds. You predicted it! YOU'RE A CLAIRVOYANT!

Clara groaned. Would it never end?

It's just a coincidence, she texted back. Then she set down the phone and stretched out on her bed, wishing Elaine were around to assure her that of course it was just a coincidence. Horoscopes were just woo.

Her phone buzzed again, and she snatched it up. Maeve had sent a dozen crystal ball emojis.

Clara tucked the phone under her pillow. She had nothing to say to that.

CHAPTER 11

ON MONDAY MORNING, A BOY STOPPED Clara on her way to her locker. He was tall and very freckled, and she was pretty sure she'd seen him stitching socks on his lunch break with the knitting club. He was also, he informed her straight away, a Scorpio.

"Are you," she said, dreading the conversation ahead. She'd spent the previous day writing another round of horoscopes, and she was now officially sick of astrology. Part of her had hoped that Mrs. Major had recycled all the *Gazette* copies in the school over the weekend. That seemed like something the custodian would do.

"Yes," said the boy. "And you predicted that I'd soon embark on a journey."

"Did I," said Clara.

The boy nodded. "And this past weekend, my dad announced that he's taking our whole family to Mexico for Christmas!"

Clara blinked at him.

"Amazing, right?"

Clara forced herself to smile. "That's a fun coincidence,"

she said, with emphasis on *coincidence*. "Have a nice trip." She stepped around him and marched on to her locker.

She found Maeve there, chatting with her friend Maddie.

"Clara!" Maddie spun to face her. "You're just the person I wanted to talk to."

"I am?" Clara braced herself again.

"The Libra horoscope you wrote. Was that for me?"

Clara shook her head. She couldn't even remember it.

"You predicted that there would be a wedding in my family. Remember?"

Clara didn't really, but she nodded so as to speed up the conversation.

"On Saturday night, my aunt announced that she got engaged! How did you do that?"

"I didn't," Clara told her. "I just made it up."

"Oh, wow!" said Maeve. "That's so cool! Clara predicted that I'd get a second audition!"

"No, I didn't!" Clara gave her a "you're not helping" look.

"Well, you kind of did."

Clara turned to her locker and shoved her backpack inside. It's not real, she reminded herself. It's just a coincidence.

"I'm going to be the flower girl, even though I think junior bridesmaid would be more appropriate for an eleven-year-old," Maddie went on. "What do you think, Clara?"

"I really have no idea," Clara said to her locker.

"Well, maybe think about it and let me know," Maddie told her. Then she waved goodbye and walked off to her class.

"Spooo-keeeeey," Maeve giggled. "This is so fun, Clara!"

Definitely not the word Clara would have chosen.

"Hey, check this out." Maeve reached into her locker and pulled out what looked like a large gray caterpillar. She pressed it to her upper lip. "Ta-da!"

"Morris Mumford?" Clara guessed.

"Morris Mumford," said Maeve. "I've got my second audition after school today, which gives me . . ." She checked her watch. "Six and a half hours to get inside the mind, body and soul of Detective Mumford."

"You're actually going to wear that all day?" asked Clara, who wouldn't have worn a mustache at school for all the guacamole in Toronto.

Maeve nodded. "I'm going to try."

"So that means you've decided to be a Morris instead of Moira or Molly," Clara said as they headed for science class.

Maeve sighed and nodded. "I'm up against Jin for the role. I figure I have to be his equal."

Clara was pretty sure there was a flaw in this logic, but before she could find it, someone called, "Hey, Clara, hold up a minute."

"Not again," Clara sighed, turning around. Which horoscope-obsessed kid wanted to talk now?

She gasped.

Wesley Ferris was striding down the hallway toward her. In a pinstriped suit.

"Oh my gosh!" Maeve squeaked.

Clara shushed her. "Oh hi, Wesley," she said, trying to sound casual. "Um, great suit."

Wesley halted in front of her, then looked from Clara to Maeve and back to Clara. She pulled her to the other side of the hallway, out of earshot.

"Oh. Um. Okay," said Clara.

"Clara." Wesley looked left and right. "I have an assignment for you."

"You *do*?" Clara cried.

Wesley shushed her.

"Sorry," Clara whispered. "I mean, that's great. I'll do it. What is it?"

Wesley looked around again, and Clara leaned in excitedly. "Mrs. Major has requested an article," said Wesley. "About the new green bins."

Clara pulled back. "The green bins."

Wesley nodded.

"Like, you want me to write about composting."

"Exactly."

Clara drew a breath. Of course her next assignment was about garbage. *Of course.* "But I thought you turned down her request."

"I did at first," said Wesley. "I don't think staff should be allowed to dictate the content of the *Gazette*. But then I reconsidered. Now that we've increased our publishing schedule, we need more articles. And waste management is an important topic."

Clara suspected that Wesley's change of heart had more to do with the custodian's reaction to her request being turned down. It probably wasn't pretty.

"So, will you do it?" asked Wesley.

"Um . . ." Clara hesitated. On one hand, it wasn't the horoscopes. On the other hand, it was an article about *composting*.

Wesley put her hands on her hips. "You said you wanted another assignment, Clara. I know you have your own column and all, but you are still a Newbie Newsy. And Newbie Newsies can't be—"

"I know," Clara cut in. "Okay, I'll do it."

"Good," said Wesley. "I'll tell Mrs. Major that you'll interview her after school today."

"Wait, what?" Clara gasped.

"*Mrs. Major?*" Maeve cried from the other side of the hallway. Wesley looked over at her. "Oops. Sorry!" Maeve waved. "Go on."

Wesley turned back to Clara. "Is that girl wearing a mustache?"

"She's getting into character," Clara explained.

Wesley shook her head. "Anyway, you have to interview Mrs. Major. The article wouldn't be complete without her. That isn't a problem, is it?"

"No." Clara swallowed hard. "No. I can do that."

"Good. We'll run it in the next issue, which means the article is actually due today. But this is pretty last-minute, so I'll give you until tomorrow evening."

"Oh. Great," said Clara. Writing an article in a day sounded like an awful lot of work. But she *had* asked for another assignment.

"Great," Wesley agreed, and she marched off, pinstriped pants swishing.

Maeve leaped across the hallway and grabbed Clara's arm. "Did she say what I think she said? You have to interview *Mrs. Major*? Clara, you might not survive! What if you go into her office and never come back out?"

"It'll be fine," Clara assured her, though she'd been thinking along the same lines.

"I'll come with you!" Maeve declared. "You won't face her alone!"

Clara shook her head and pulled her arm back. "You have your audition today. Remember?" She poked Maeve's mustache. It felt like a small, dead rodent. She shuddered.

"Oh, right." Maeve smoothed her mustache. "I'll skip it."

"No, you won't. That's crazy." Clara pulled her on toward science class.

"Well, then let's meet up after your interview and my audition," said Maeve. "If you don't show up, I'll send out a search party. We'll scour the dumpster for your remains!"

"Ew, Maeve!" Clara made a face. "That's awful."

Maeve nodded. "I know. But my dad and I watched this crime show last night, and two cops were searching this dark alley, and one heard a tapping sound in the dumpster, and then they—"

"Maeve!" Clara snapped. "Not helping!"

"Sorry," said Maeve. "I'll stop."

"Thank you," said Clara, and she shuddered again.

☄

Never before had she willed a school day to slow down. But time passed as usual—possibly even faster than usual—as Clara awaited her interview with Mrs. Major. When the bell rang at the end of the day, she steeled her nerves, grabbed her notebook and headed for the custodian's office, half hoping Mrs. Major had forgotten all about their interview and had already gone home.

Where *was* Mrs. Major's home? she wondered as she approached the custodian's door. It had never occurred to her that she even had one.

Not only that, she realized as she knocked, but Mrs. Major was a *Mrs.*! She was *married*! Did she have *children*? Was that even *possible*?

The door swung open, and Clara found herself at eye level with the custodian's biceps. She jumped back.

"You're the reporter!" barked Mrs. Major.

"Y-y-yes, ma'am," Clara stammered. "I'm Clara. Hi. Um, should we do the interview . . . here?" She peered around Mrs. Major into her office.

"No." Mrs. Major slammed the door shut behind her, and Clara jumped again. "I'll take you straight to the scene of the crime."

"Oh. Okay," Clara said, relieved that she wouldn't have to enter the custodian's office and risk never coming back out. Except now every kid at KMS would see her hanging out with Mrs. Major after school. But the custodian was already marching off down the hallway, so Clara had no choice but to hurry after her.

"Um, can I ask you some questions?" Clara asked as they marched down the hallway.

"Well, this is an interview!" Mrs. Major boomed.

"Right. Okay." Clara looked at her list of what Wesley called "warm-up questions." They were simple and quick, designed to make the interview subject comfortable before delving into the hard-hitting questions that mattered. "Can I get your full name?"

"What for?" Mrs. Major snapped.

"Um, well, it is a newspaper article," said Clara.

"Melinda Major!"

Melinda. Clara scribbled this down. She'd never have guessed. "Birthday?"

"February seventh," Mrs. Major snapped. "And the year is none of your business."

"No problem." Clara noted this, and then decided to go ahead and ask an impromptu question. "Do you . . . have children?"

Mrs. Major snorted. "I put up with enough of you at work."

"Fair enough," said Clara. "Hobbies?"

"Here we are!" Mrs. Major stopped suddenly beside the recycling station outside the cafeteria doors. She flipped up the lid of a green bin and motioned for Clara to look inside. There, atop a mound of banana peels and apple cores, lay the evidence.

"It's a juice box," Clara observed.

"It's a *crime*," said Mrs. Major.

"I see." Clearly Mrs. Major hadn't watched nearly as many crime shows as Maeve. Clara took a few notes: *Juice box.*

Tropical punch. She snapped a photo with her phone. "So, how often do you come across these . . . crime scenes?"

"Every single day." Mrs. Major plucked it out of the green bin and tossed it into a blue box for recycling. Then she closed the green bin and lifted it up onto her shoulder as if it weighed nothing at all. She strode off again, and Clara followed.

"You have no idea what I put up with," Mrs. Major assured her. "I'll give you a full list of compostable items—you'll definitely want to include that in your article." She hung a left down another hallway, in which three boys were tossing a Frisbee. They froze at the sight of her, then scattered.

"Well, okay," Clara said, though it didn't sound like much of a story.

"The point of composting is to break down organic matter into a rich soil. Plastics and metals don't biodegrade—they stick around for thousands of years. Thousands! Note that," Mrs. Major instructed. Clara did.

"So if I find a bin that's packed with contaminants, I'll just throw it in the garbage." Mrs. Major pushed open a door and strode outside to the staff parking lot. "Which means that all our efforts to cut down on waste were for nothing! Nobody wins with contaminated bins!"

Nobody wins with contaminated bins. Clara noted this too. It had headline potential.

Mrs. Major led her to a green container nearly as tall as Clara. She lifted the lid and dumped in the contents of her bin before peering inside.

"Most people don't realize that a healthy compost is like

a work of art," said Mrs. Major. "You want the perfect balance of greens and browns. Nice, rich tones, like olive and moss, ocher and russet." Her face seemed to soften, just a little bit.

Olive and moss, ocher and russet. Clara scribbled this down. It reminded her of her mother's vast collection of paint chips. She stepped up to the bin for a peek.

"No!" Mrs. Major slammed the lid shut.

"Whoa!" Clara stumbled backward, dropping her notebook and pen.

"It smells," Mrs. Major said quickly.

Weird, Clara thought, bending to gather her things. But she wasn't about to argue—she didn't want to see the compost that badly. "Maybe you could . . ." She motioned for Mrs. Major to stand in front of the bin for a photo, and the custodian obliged, setting her fists on her hips.

"Perfect," Clara said, and she snapped the photo.

Mrs. Major led her back to the office, where she told Clara to wait outside while she found a full list of compostable materials, titled "Mrs. Major's Composting Dos and Don'ts." "That should be all you need," she said when she reemerged. "But let me know if you have any more questions. This is an important article. A front-page feature, I'd say."

Clara nodded, though she knew it would get buried between the lunch specials and the classified ads. She thanked Mrs. Major for her time, and the custodian nodded. Then she slipped back into her office and slammed the door.

CHAPTER 12

"I DON'T KNOW WHAT CAME OVER

me," Maeve recounted the next day as they left science class. "There I was, walking up to the stage, when I just felt this . . . this *urge*. I ripped off that awful mustache, tossed it into the front row and marched onto the stage as Detective Molly Mumford! Ms. Flynn was shocked. Clara, you should have seen her face. But I think the audition went pretty well. In fact, I'd say . . ." She paused. "Hey, are you okay?"

"Me?" said Clara. "Oh yeah. Sure."

"You seem out of sorts," Maeve observed. "A little narky—that's what my mom would say."

Clara *was* feeling out of sorts—she'd been feeling that way since she woke up, after staying up late to write her article, "Nobody Wins with Contaminated Bins." At breakfast, Gaby had insisted on tossing a spoonful of mugwort in her cereal, to perk her up. Clara could now say for certain that mugwort didn't belong in cereal either.

"I'm fine," she told Maeve. "But actually, I have to go." She pointed to the girls' washroom down the hall.

"I'd better too," Maeve said, pushing the door open. "So anyway, I think the audition went . . . Whoa." She ground to a halt.

Three eighth grade girls standing at the sinks turned to glare at them. Clara took a step back and then froze at the sight of the girl in the middle. It was Olivia Silva, and her cheeks were streaked with tears and mascara.

"Um, we'll go someplace else." Clara began to shuffle back out, but stopped when Olivia pointed a finger at her.

"You!"

Maeve and Clara looked at each other, and then back at the older girl. "Sorry?"

"Clara Voyant! That's you, isn't it?"

Oh no, thought Clara. Not the KMS Fashionista too!

"This is your fault!" Olivia cried.

"What?" Maeve looked at Clara. "What's she talking about?"

"You write the horoscopes, don't you?"

Clara nodded, wishing very much that she'd faked sick that morning. She wondered if the Counterfeit Kid was still selling his forged doctors' notes.

"Well, they're terrible," Olivia sniffled. "At least mine was. I did what you told me to do, and it was awful advice!"

Clara's mouth fell open. "You . . . what?"

"Olivia is a Leo," one of her friends explained. "Your horoscope advised her to speak her mind, assert herself like the lion she is. So she told a boy that she likes him. And . . . it didn't go well." The girl bit her lip and glanced at Olivia.

"He ran away!" Olivia wailed.

"No!" cried Maeve.

"That's . . . that's unbelievable!" said Clara.

"I know," Olivia sniffed. "But he did."

"I meant that you took my advice," Clara said. Maeve poked her in the ribs.

But it *was* unbelievable. And utterly ridiculous. Who in their right mind would take horoscopes so seriously?

"Olivia, that boy is a bonehead," Maeve told her.

"But he isn't," she said, wiping her eyes with a wad of toilet paper. "He's an artist. Maybe a Pisces?" She looked at her friend, who shrugged. Olivia turned to Clara. "What's in store for Pisces?"

"You've got to be kidding me," muttered Clara.

"Preston is definitely a Pisces," the other friend piped up. "Remember, his party was on St. Patrick's Day last year—"

"Wait, *Preston*?" shouted Maeve.

Olivia shushed her, as if there were any way Preston could hear them.

"Preston?" Maeve repeated in a whisper. "Why?"

Olivia's friend glared at Maeve and then turned back to Olivia. "He likes you, Ollie. Of course he does. He wouldn't have taken all those photos of you if he didn't. Also, you featured him on *KMS Fashionista*, which has totally helped build his personal brand."

Clara couldn't take any more. She turned to leave.

"Clara, wait," said Olivia. "When does the next round of horoscopes come out?"

"Next Friday," Clara sighed.

"Well, I need a better one, okay? And a good one for Pisces too."

This is insane, thought Clara. What's more, she'd already written the next round of horoscopes, once again with Paquito in mind for Leo. She'd suggested he needed a new strategy for dealing with his health issues, which was solid advice for Paquito, but clearly not for Olivia. But it was too late to change it. "Look, the thing is—" she began.

"Good," Olivia said. "I'm counting on you, Clara. Don't take this lightly." She turned and disappeared into a stall, shutting the door behind her.

☄

"First order of business," Wesley began once all the Newsies were present at that Tuesday's after-school meeting. "Let's discuss the last issue: what feedback have you gotten from our readers?"

"People love the horoscopes!" Lizzie declared.

Clara groaned inwardly. Couldn't everyone just *stop*?

"I think they're actually more popular than the forgery story!" said Matt.

"No." Clara shook her head. "That can't be true."

"Actually, I think it is," said Ravi. He didn't seem upset about it.

"Maybe next time the horoscopes should go on the front page," Lina suggested as she doodled a swirl of stars and planets in her sketchbook.

"No!" Clara and Wesley cried in unison.

"Absolutely not," Wesley added.

"But they came true!" Lizzie insisted. "Ooh, can you show us the horoscopes for the next issue? I want to know what the universe has in store."

Clara put her head in her hands.

"Okay, Newsies, this has gone far enough." Wesley thumped the table. "Horoscopes are *not real*. And if you think they are, you're not thinking critically. And if you're not thinking critically, you're not being a good journalist."

Clara lifted her head and nodded gratefully.

"But there has to be some truth to it," Lizzie argued. "My horoscope description is really accurate. The Taurus is dependable and patient and a really good cook."

Wesley rolled her eyes. "I'm a Taurus too, you know."

Lizzie gaped. "You are?"

Wesley nodded. "And I hate cooking."

"And she's definitely not patient," Lina murmured.

Wesley glared at Lina, and then turned back to Lizzie. "That's called subjective validation."

"Subjective what?"

"Subjective validation," Wesley repeated slowly, enunciating each syllable. "That's when two things are thought to be related because of a prior expectation."

"Come again?" said Ravi.

"English, please," Lina added.

Wesley let out a long-suffering sigh. "Okay, let's say Lizzie reads a description of a Taurus, and she thinks it fits her perfectly. But even before she read it, she *believed* that it would fit her perfectly. She'd basically made up her mind ahead of time. That's subjective validation."

"How do you know that?" Ravi asked.

Wesley sniffed. "I read."

Subjective validation. Clara repeated the phrase to herself. She'd never heard of it before, but it sounded like a good explanation, especially coming from Wesley. It made her feel a bit better about the whole situation.

Subjective validation. She scribbled the words in her notebook, along with the definition. After everything that had happened that day, she was pretty sure she'd need it.

⬨

"It's subjective validation," she told Gaby and Maeve later that afternoon.

"Sub–what now?" said Maeve, who was sitting beside her at the counter in Healing Herbs, sipping a lavender-lousewort tea. Across from them, Gaby was concocting a poultice for Sophie, who had a swollen wrist from too much scooping.

"It's like this," Clara said, trying to recall Wesley's words without checking her notes. "When you guys read the description of a Gemini—"

"We're very social, you know," Gaby said, shaking some bright-yellow arnica leaves into her mortar and mashing them with her pestle.

"And adventurous," added Maeve.

"Don't forget adaptable," said Gaby.

"Charming too," said Maeve. They shared a smile.

Clara seethed silently. "*Anyway*, when you guys read the description of a Gemini, you think it fits you perfectly. But that's only because you believed in it *before* you read it. Basically, you would have believed whatever it said, even if it told you Geminis were, like, really bad dancers or something."

Maeve and Gaby exchanged skeptical looks.

"I think Geminis are actually renowned for their dance moves," said Gaby. She snapped her fingers and shimmied her hips to some song in her head.

"Totally." Maeve swayed on her stool, as if she could hear it too.

Clara let out a long-suffering sigh, à la Wesley Ferris. There really was no hope.

"I have an idea!" said Gaby. "I'll post the horoscopes right here on the counter, so that customers can read them while they wait for their remedies." She pulled a copy of the *Gazette* out of a drawer and set it down beside her mortar and pestle.

"Great idea," Maeve said, checking her watch. "Oh! I have to go. I have a date with my dad to watch *The World's Creepiest Criminals*." She slid off her stool. "Thanks for the tea, Gaby! Bye, Clara!" And she dashed out of the store.

"I really like her," Gaby said as the door swung shut. "Have I mentioned that?"

"You have," said Clara.

"She's a good friend. I'm glad you're making friends. Does it make you feel more settled here?"

Clara shrugged. She didn't really want to talk about it.

"But it's grown on you a bit, right? Our new life, I mean." Her mother looked hopeful.

Before Clara could reply, Gaby's phone rang. She checked the caller. "It's Lily! Mind if I take it?"

"Please do," Clara said, glad to put that conversation on hold. She took the opportunity to text her grandmother again.

Now can you talk? she asked Elaine.

"Ooh, fun," her mother said to the phone. "How could I say no to Mystic Mart?"

Clara shuddered. She could easily think of a hundred different ways.

Her phone buzzed with a text from Elaine. I have watercolor class tonight, dear. It starts in fifteen minutes. Another time?

"*Watercolor class?*" Clara said to the phone. "But that involves, like, colors!"

What had Florida done to Elaine? She'd never been one for learning new—

Clara nearly dropped her phone as a thought came to mind. She grabbed her mother's copy of the *Gazette* and flipped to the back page.

You've gone through some big changes lately, Virgo. And you might be feeling a bit unsettled. Joining a class or learning a new skill could help you meet new people and find your groove.

She dropped the paper and gripped her stool. It's a *coincidence*, she told herself again. It had to be. Horoscopes weren't real, and she couldn't predict the future.

"You can't predict the future," she told herself aloud.

Could she?

"No," she said to herself. "That's ridiculous."

CHAPTER 13

"**I CANNOT BELIEVE YOU LEFT IT** this long," Maeve said as they walked up the steps to her house on Friday afternoon.

"I've been busy," Clara told her, though it wasn't really true. She knew it wasn't best-friend-y to lie, but she wasn't sure she could tell Maeve the truth about Halloween.

"But it's the most important day of the year!" cried Maeve. "It's—"

"Ladies!" Mr. Healy-Lin flung the door open just as Maeve touched the handle. Clara and Maeve shrieked in surprise, and then shrieked again at the sight of his apron, which appeared to be splattered with blood.

"Tomato sauce," said Mr. Healy-Lin.

They sighed with relief.

"Come in, come in!" He ushered them inside. "Clara Costa! So glad you could join us for dinner."

Gaby had sent a text around lunchtime that day: I have to run errands with Lily this evening. Want to have dinner at Maeve's? I checked with her dad and he said yes.

Errands with Lily? Clara couldn't believe it. Her mother was choosing errands with Lily over their Friday night taco ritual! That stung.

But as she stepped into the Healy-Lin house, all the resentment slipped away. Because Maeve's home, as usual, was perfectly, delightfully, gloriously *normal*.

"What's for dinner?" Maeve asked as she hung up her coat. Clara did the same, noting how nice it was to enter a house without passing through a curtain of beads.

"It's a surprise." Mr. Healy-Lin led them through the foyer and into the kitchen.

"It has tomato sauce in it," Clara pointed out, noting how nice it was to know that the tomato sauce would not contain mugwort.

"Pizza?" Maeve guessed.

"Nope," said Mr. Healy-Lin.

"Spaghetti."

"Uh-uh."

While Maeve went on guessing, Clara took a seat at the kitchen counter and admired her surroundings. Not only was the Healy-Lin house easily five times the size of her and Gaby's apartment, it was clean and orderly. Every wall was painted a creamy vanilla, so when you went to the bathroom, you didn't feel like you were trapped inside a tropical fruit. The radiators didn't need to be kicked, and there wasn't a single squirrel nesting in the roof.

She breathed it all in, wishing she could stay forever.

"Aha!" Maeve pointed triumphantly at a box of noodles on the counter. "Lasagna!"

"Excellent detective skills, Mumford," said her father. "And chocolate cupcakes for dessert."

"My favorites." Maeve's eyes widened. "Is it my birthday? Did I forget?"

"Nutbar," Clara poked her. "You're a—" She stopped herself before she uttered the word "Gemini." There would be no talk of horoscopes in the Healy-Lin household.

"My half-birthday?"

Mr. Healy-Lin shook his head as he peeled a carrot for the salad. "But it is a day for celebration."

Maeve tapped her chin. "Did you get a raise?" Her father was an accountant—a delightfully normal profession. That had been Elaine's second choice of career, after government statistician.

"No, it's not about me." He set down his vegetable peeler. "I received an important phone call around noon today. You, my dear, have been awarded the role of Detective Mumford in *The Seventh Slipper: A Molly Mumford Mystery*."

Maeve's mouth fell open. "*Really?*"

"Really." Her father smiled.

"Molly Mumford!" Clara cried. "Maeve, you did it!"

Maeve sat for another minute, looking stunned. Then she leaped off her chair and punched the air. "I did it! Oh my gosh, does Mom know yet?"

Mr. Healy-Lin shook his head. "She's at a rehearsal tonight, but I don't think it's started yet." He handed her the phone.

Maeve grabbed it and ran upstairs. Moments later, they heard her squeal, "I did it, I did it, I did it!" Then she launched into a tap dance.

Mr. Healy-Lin resumed peeling carrots. "Ms. Flynn plans to post the audition results at school on Monday morning, but she wanted Maeve to have the weekend to . . ." He looked up at the ceiling. Maeve's tapping continued.

"Dance it out?" Clara finished. It was a smart move on Ms. Flynn's part.

"Exactly," said Mr. Healy-Lin. "Anyway, I hear you predicted this."

Clara sighed. "You don't need to be a clairvoyant to know that Maeve will be a star," she said. And her stomach pinched again—just a little bit.

Mr. Healy-Lin stopped chopping and looked at her for a moment. She felt her face flush. Could he tell how much she envied Maeve's success? "Maeve tells me you've been trying to get a better assignment at the *Gazette*," he said. "Any luck?"

She shrugged. "I wrote one about compost bins."

He nodded. "Waste management is an important topic."

"Yeah," said Clara.

"Things will get better, you know. Your editor—what's her name? Wendy?"

"Wesley."

"Right. Wesley's graduating this year, isn't she?"

Clara nodded, impressed that Maeve's dad bothered to remember these things. He had some excellent friend skills too—possibly it was genetic. "She's going to an arts-focused high school with a good journalism program next year. So she can really get serious about her career as a newspaper editor."

His mouth twitched. "Well then, next year you'll have a different editor, and they'll give you better assignments," he assured her. "They'll have to, because you're an excellent writer. You even managed to make that knitting article interesting. That was no easy feat." He pointed his carrot peeler at her.

She mustered a smile. "Thanks."

And yet, it was only October; Wesley's graduation felt like a long way off. In the meantime, Clara had a whole lot of horoscopes to write, not to mention a whole lot of kids who seemed to believe they were coming true. Which they weren't. It was just a co—

"So Halloween is on Monday! What's your costume?" Mr. Healy-Lin asked brightly, clearly trying to change the subject.

"Oh. I'm not sure yet," said Clara. "I'm working on it," she added, though she hadn't given it any thought. The truth was, she didn't really like Halloween. Except for the part about collecting candy—that she could get behind. But the rest of it kind of creeped her out.

And she had more than enough creepiness in her life right now.

Back when she lived with Elaine, Clara would often return home from trick-or-treating to find the duplex completely dark. That was Elaine's way of dissuading trick-or-treaters from coming to the door. And if they still insisted on it, she'd make everyone stay very quiet and still until they left. This drove Gaby bonkers, since (surprise, surprise) she adored Halloween. This year, she'd decorated Healing Herbs from floor to ceiling with cobwebs and black streamers.

Maeve thundered down the stairs. "I! Am! So! Excited!" she yelled. "And Clara Voyant, you *know* what this means!"

"It means you are an excellent actress," her father said, plopping the steaming dish of lasagna on the table. "Now let's eat."

♆

Clara let herself in by the back door of Healing Herbs, then turned to wave at Mr. Healy-Lin in his Volvo. He was leaning over the steering wheel, looking concerned. Possibly he wasn't used to dropping his daughter's friends off in dark, rat-infested back alleys. Clara waved one more time to assure him she was fine, and then closed the door and bolted it shut.

She could have flicked on the lights but didn't, instead feeling her way through the storeroom and over to the staircase. Then she climbed up the steps to the sour-smelling hallway and let herself into the apartment, already missing the Healy-Lin household.

"Mom?" she said, stepping through the beaded curtain.

"In here!" Gaby called from the living room. "How was dinner?"

"Good." Clara dumped her backpack near the door and hung her coat on the rack. "Maeve got her part in the play, so we had lasagna and cupcakes to celebrate, and—What are you doing?"

Her mother was sitting cross-legged on the floor, with the laptop in her lap and papers strewn around her.

"Accounting?" Clara guessed.

Gaby looked up and tilted her head to the side, as if she'd never heard of the word.

Clara sighed. "Never mind."

"Come sit with me." Gaby patted the floor beside her. "I've made the most amazing discovery! Oh, and congrats to Maeve—that's wonderful news! Also, you predicted it!"

Clara frowned. She didn't feel like sitting on the floor, but her mother patted it again, harder this time. So she sank down beside her.

"So I was perusing *Witchipedia*," Gaby began.

"You mean *Wikipedia*."

"No, *Witchipedia*." Gaby pointed to the webpage open on the laptop. "It's an online encyclopedia, but for witches."

"That is not a thing," Clara said flatly.

"Is too." Gaby shifted the laptop so she could see the webpage, which was, in fact, titled *Witchipedia*. "And here's the craziest part: I came upon the page for Flavia McGrath!"

"Crazy," Clara said. "I don't know who that is."

"My great-aunt!" Gaby cried. "She's a real-life witch! She has a *Witchipedia* page!"

"No," said Clara.

"Yes!" Gaby pushed the laptop at her again. "Look!"

Clara peered at the page. Under the heading "Flavia McGrath" was a photo of an elderly, white-haired woman. She was staring at the camera as if willing it to burst into flames.

Flavia McGrath (born Feb. 6, 1930) is a writer, researcher and practicing witch. Originally from Toronto, Canada, she currently resides on the Isle of Wight, where she leads the White Raven Coven.

The article went on to list over a dozen articles and books Flavia had written.

"We're related to her?" Clara inched away from the laptop.

"She's Elaine's aunt, so my great-aunt and your great-great-aunt. She's pretty old now—this photo must have been taken a few decades ago."

"So why have I never heard of this . . . person?" asked Clara.

"Oh, I'm sure I mentioned her at some point," said Gaby. "But you know Elaine. Flavia isn't her kind of person. She wasn't a big fan."

Probably the understatement of the year, thought Clara. She squinted at the photo. Flavia and Elaine did share the same small, sharp nose and thin lips. And Clara had seen that same fiery look on Elaine's face—like when trick-or-treaters approached their front door, or when she found Gaby wearing the technicolor-swirl skirt after she'd garbaged it for the sixth time.

But a witch? In the *family*?

"I'd forgotten about Flavia until I went to Mystic Mart tonight with Lily. Oh my gosh, Cee, Mystic Mart is incredible! You'll have to come with us next time. Anyway, I came across one of her books." Gaby picked up a paperback from the floor and handed it to Clara.

"*A Witch's Grimoire*," Clara read. She didn't know what a grimoire was and didn't want to ask. The lasagna and cupcakes in her stomach began to roil.

"It's like a witch's manual, or textbook," Gaby explained, grinning. "Can you believe it? We're related to a witch! Maybe you get your powers of clairvoyance from her!"

Clara put down the book. She wanted to tell her mother, in no uncertain terms, that she didn't have powers of clairvoyance. She wanted to say that she was pretty sure horoscopes and witchcraft were two very different things. She wanted to point out that *Witchipedia* was at best a questionable source of information, and that her mother needed to stop believing everything she read on the Internet.

Instead, she said, "I'm going to bed." And she stood up and walked to her room.

"Wait, come back!" called Gaby. "You have to read about the members of Flavia's coven! These people are wild!" Then she gasped. "Cee! We should go to the Isle of Wight to visit them! Wouldn't that be incredible? Hmm, I wonder where the Isle of Wight is."

Clara didn't answer. She marched to her room, shut her door and buried herself under her blankets to block out the world.

"HOW ABOUT THIS?" MAEVE HELD
up a pair of denim bell-bottoms. "You could be a hippie from the '60s! We'd get you a tie-dyed T-shirt to go with it. I'm pretty sure your mom has one. Oh! And you'd wear these!" She grabbed a pair of big, round sunglasses from the pile and handed them to Clara.

Clara wrinkled her nose and set the glasses down. "Those jeans smell like someone died in them." Actually, most things in the secondhand clothing shop smelled like that.

Maeve shrugged. "It's possible." She folded them and set them back on the pile. "I still can't believe it's the day before Halloween and you don't have a costume. Clara, this is bonkers!"

"We'll find something." Clara picked up a tutu and checked the seams for bedbugs. Or not, she thought, setting it back down. If they didn't find her a costume, she could just stay home and turn out all the lights. But then, she'd miss out on the candy. She picked up a curly red wig and then set it back down too.

"Maybe we can find you a police costume," Maeve suggested. "Then we could be a team: Detective Molly Mumford and Inspector Clara Voyant. Ooh, that has a nice ring to it."

Clara hummed in agreement, though it sounded like a lot of effort. She picked up a black-and-purple-striped T-shirt long enough to be a dress. It reminded her of something, so she studied it for a moment.

Finally it came to her. "Buzzter!" She turned to Maeve. "I know! I'll be Buzzter the Honeybee!" She held up the T-shirt dress. "I'll just wear this and some black leggings."

"Good find," Maeve said. "And let's get some pipe cleaners and a headband, and make you antennae."

Clara checked the price tag: three dollars—she could handle that. She quickly turned the T-shirt inside out to check for bedbugs but couldn't find any.

"I wonder what happened to him," Maeve said as Clara paid for the shirt. "Buzzter, I mean. You'd have solved that mystery if Wesley had let you."

Clara nodded, counting out her change and handing it to the cashier.

"I wonder if he's being held prisoner somewhere. What if they're torturing him?" Maeve whispered.

"Maeve, he's a piñata." Clara tucked her costume into her backpack.

"Still." Maeve shook her head. "It's a cruel world."

They were headed out the door when Maeve suddenly froze. "Clara!"

Clara stopped just short of walking into her. "What?"

"You could find him! Buzzter!"

"Maeve, we've been over this," she said impatiently. "Wesley said I'm not allowed to—"

"No!" Maeve gripped her arm. "I mean you could use your powers of clairvoyance to find him! I saw it on TV once: the detectives brought in this psychic to find a girl who'd been kidnapped in the parking lot of her school!"

"I'm not even going to answer that," Clara told her, pulling her outside.

"I'm just saying," Maeve said as they hopped down the steps to Kensington Avenue. "It could make your work a lot easier. Maybe you could predict stories before they even happen!"

Clara snorted. "Right."

She had to admit, though, that it was kind of tempting, using her powers to find a really good *Gazette* story.

Not that she had powers.

But . . . if she did.

"Just think about it," Maeve advised.

"Sure," said Clara. "Right."

❦

On Monday night, Gaby closed up shop early because, as she explained, "Halloween is basically a holiday."

Once again, Clara had her doubts but didn't argue. Her mother planned to cook her a pre-trick-or-treating dinner, which Clara would hastily consume before Maeve and her dad came to pick her up at six o'clock. They'd head for the Annex neighborhood near the university, which Maeve claimed was their best bet for candy collection. Apparently she'd done extensive research.

Clara had just changed into her Buzzter costume and was adjusting her antennae when she heard a knock at the apartment door. Trick-or-treaters? she wondered. But that was impossible; they would have to come through the shop. Had Gaby forgotten to lock up?

"Door's open!" her mother yelled from the kitchen, where she was making pumpkin soup.

Clara froze. She didn't like the sound of this.

The beaded curtain rustled. "Sweet pea!"

"No!" Clara groaned. She tossed her antennae aside and stomped out of her room to show her mother exactly how she felt about her inviting Lily over without consulting her. But Gaby was too busy tossing herbs into her soup to notice.

"Clara!" Lily pranced over to hug her. "Oh, sweet pea, your home is adorable!"

Clara wiggled out of her arms. Lily was wearing her usual black lace dress, but today she'd added a crown of snakes on her head. "Are those *real*?" Clara recoiled.

Lily nodded, and the snakes bobbed their heads along with her. "But don't worry. They died of natural causes."

"Happy Halloween!" Terence peeked through the beaded curtain.

Clara gasped. Terence's face was ghostly white, with thick black circles around his eyes and black lines around his lips. On his forehead was an intricate black spiderweb.

"Pretty great, right?" he said. "Lily painted it. She's so talented."

"Oh, sweet pea." Lily untangled him from the beads.

"You guys look amazing!" said Gaby. "I'm so glad you could come. We have so much to celebrate!"

"Totally," said Terence. "I made us kombucha!" He pulled a bottle of cloudy amber liquid out of a grocery bag.

"What is that?" Clara grimaced, just as her mother cried, "Wonderful!" Gaby shot her a "be polite" look.

"Fermented tea," said Lily.

"It's delicious," Gaby said, stirring her soup. "You'll like it, Cee."

Clara highly doubted that.

"Terence, sweet pea, look at the beautiful colors in here!" Lily was wandering around the kitchen, wide-eyed. "I feel like I'm swimming in a jar of pasta sauce."

"Or a vat of blood!" Terence added. Then he laughed demonically, and Lily joined in. The snakes on her head bobbed and writhed.

Clara tried once again to imagine what Elaine would do if she were there. She'd probably toss Terence and Lily out the window. And send the kombucha flying out after them. Clara wished she could do that herself.

"Hey, Mom, maybe I'll just walk over to Maeve's early," she said.

"Without dinner? No way." Gaby shook her head. "The soup is ready, so let's eat now. Can you set the table, Cee?"

Clara sighed. "Fine."

"That sounds great, Gabs," said Lily. "Then we can get down to business."

"What kind of business?" Clara asked, grabbing spoons from the drawer.

"Oh, didn't I tell you?" Gaby said as she tossed some salt in her soup. "We're having a séance."

The spoons clattered to the floor.

"Just a little one." Lily put a hand on Clara's shoulder. "Nothing major."

"Just a little séance?" Clara repeated. "Just, like, a *little* communing with the dead?"

Terence and Lily nodded. The snakes nodded too.

"Are you kidding me," Clara muttered, bending to pick up the spoons. She tossed them on the table without wiping them.

"It's actually a warm-up for me," said Terence. "I'm leading a big séance at the Black Cat Café later tonight. We're expecting a few dozen people—it'll be a doozy." He began to pour kombucha into four glasses. "Anyway, Clara, I really want to chat with the ghost in your bathroom."

"I'm sorry, what?" She sank into a chair. It wobbled dangerously.

"The ghost." He handed her a glass of cloudy brown liquid. "In the bathroom."

"Right." She set the glass down. "What are you talking about."

"Oh, don't you know about him?" Terence looked surprised. "Well, don't worry. I'm pretty sure he's friendly. Actually, I think he's got a great sense of humor." He chuckled, as if remembering a joke they'd shared. "But I want to make good and sure. I won't have our new friends living in a house with a menacing spirit!"

"Isn't he a hero?" Lily gushed.

Clara turned to her mother. "And you weren't going to tell me about this?"

"I didn't want to worry you." Gaby handed her a bowl of pumpkin soup and kissed her forehead. "I know you're not crazy about ghosts."

"Is anyone?" Clara cried. "I mean, besides him." She jerked her thumb at Terence, who had his nose in his glass of kombucha and was inhaling deeply.

"Clara!" Her mother frowned.

"Sorry, but . . . but this is really weird." Clara sat back on her wobbly chair. "I've never seen or heard anything in the bathroom. Except for the squirrels, but they live in the roof."

Gaby nodded. "But Terence is a professional—he senses things we don't. Anyway, you heard him: it's probably a friendly ghost. Now eat your soup. I threw in a good dose of horehound, for protection from menacing spirits. It is Halloween, after all."

Clara opened her mouth to argue again, then shut it. There was no talking sense into these people. Once again, the only way out was through; she'd just gulp down her soup and get out before the séance started.

"I propose a toast!" Terence held up his glass. "To Halloween!"

"And the end of Mercury in retrograde," Gaby added, raising her glass too. "Thank goodness that's over!"

"And to new discoveries!" Lily cried. "Like this little clairvoyant's talents." She leaned over and ruffled Clara's hair.

Clara shook her off. "I'm not a clairvoyant," she said. "And I don't have talents."

"Mm-hmm." Lily gave her a knowing look. "So how are things at school? Have you achieved celebrity status, like I predicted?"

"No," Clara said. Although now that she thought about it, more kids were talking to her than ever before. But that didn't make her a celebrity. Olivia Silva was a celebrity. Jin the dinosaur guy was a celebrity. Clara was just . . . Clara.

"Some kids think their horoscopes came true," she told Lily. "But they're wrong. It's just subjective validation."

"Is it?" Lily sipped her soup.

"Yes," said Clara. "It's ridiculous. One of them even made a terrible decision based on a fortune I wrote. Believing in horoscopes is dangerous." She threw that one at her mother.

"Being an astrologer is a tough job," Terence said. "You might even have the toughest job of anyone on the *Gazette* staff."

"I wouldn't say that," said Clara.

"No, really," he insisted. "It's a lot of pressure because you're giving people news about themselves. And everyone loves to read about themselves."

Clara had to admit he had a point. The KMS kids seemed especially interested in their own fates and fortunes.

"Well, I'm a believer," Gaby chirped. "And I'm excited about my own horoscope. Career success is in the stars for me!"

"But that's exactly the problem!" Clara cried, pointing her spoon at her mother. "That's not a real horoscope. I wrote that specifically for Maeve, not anyone else."

"Oh." Gaby looked disappointed.

"Sorry," Clara added, lowering her spoon.

"So did Maeve achieve some career success?" Lily asked.

"Well, yes," Clara admitted. "She got the lead role in a play. But *not* because of my horoscope—because she's a great actress!"

"Hmm." Lily's eyes narrowed. "Can I see the horoscopes?"

Before Clara could object, Gaby whipped out a copy of the *Gazette* and handed it over.

"What, do you just keep that on you all the time?" Clara asked her.

Gaby shrugged. "I still believe my career success is coming."

Lily looked up from the paper. "How did you write these?"

Clara sighed. "I just made them up. Unless I knew someone who had a particular sign—then I wrote a horoscope specifically for that person. Like Maeve."

Lily nodded. "So you really concentrated on the person?"

"I don't know. Maybe?" Clara shrugged.

Lily passed the paper to Terence and pointed.

"Wait, no!" Clara cried, suddenly remembering the horoscope she'd written for him.

But Terence had already read it. "Whoa!" he exclaimed. "When did you write this?"

Clara swallowed. "A few weeks ago."

"With Terence in mind?" Lily asked.

Clara didn't want to admit it, but neither could she deny it. She drew a deep breath and looked to her mother for help, but Gaby was watching Lily.

Lily nodded, sipping her soup. "Here's what I think is happening," she said, setting down her spoon. "Clara is not an astrologer."

"*Thank* you!" said Clara.

"But she could still be a clairvoyant."

"What? No!"

"Just hear me out," said Lily. "I think you can see into the mind, spirit and future of one person, if you concentrate on them. That's what I do too, when I tell fortunes. Sometimes it helps if I hold a meaningful belonging of theirs, like a scarf or a set of keys. I did that last week for Sophie," she added. "I just had this feeling something important was going to happen to her, so I held her ice cream scoop, and it came to me."

"What?" Gaby leaned forward.

"Two of her freezers were about to break down," said Lily. "She needed to fix them, and fast. Together we saved two dozen quarts of double-chocolate."

"Wow," Gaby breathed.

"Now who's the hero?" Terence beamed.

They were all completely insane, Clara decided. And she was officially done with this conversation. She stood up and took her bowl to the sink.

"I wish I had powers," Gaby sighed.

Terence and Lily exchanged a look. "Now?" asked Terence.

"Now what?" said Gaby.

Terence jumped up, ran to the door and slipped out. A moment later he returned, carrying a giant box.

"What is that?" Clara demanded. She looked at her mother, but Gaby looked just as puzzled. Terence hauled it over and placed it at her feet.

"It's a gift!" Lily squealed. "For both of you!"

"Really?" Gaby leaned over. "Want to help me, Cee?"

Clara shook her head. She had a bad feeling about the box. If its contents were alive, she wanted to be nowhere near it.

Lily danced in her chair while Gaby pried open the lid. "You're going to love it! When you made your big discovery the other day, Terence and I just knew you had to have one!"

Gaby gasped. "Oh my goodness, you guys!"

"What is it?" Clara asked, craning her neck to see.

Gaby hauled a giant pot out of the box. It looked very old and a little crusty, like the kind of pot you'd see in a movie about—

"Oh *no*," Clara whispered.

"A cauldron! You guys!" Gaby looked up at her friends, eyes shiny with tears. "This is the greatest gift ever!"

"What?" Clara looked from Lily to Terence to her mother. "Why?"

"We know the discovery of Flavia McGrath meant so much to you, Gabs," said Lily. "Who knows? You might have some untapped powers, just like Clara."

"I don't have powers!" Clara cried, but they were too focused on the cauldron to hear her.

The *cauldron*. They'd bought her mother a *cauldron*.

It was more than Clara could take. She left her bowl in the sink and marched off to her room, where she grabbed her antennae and a pillowcase for trick-or-treating. Then she headed for the door, to wait for Maeve and her father outside.

She didn't say goodbye, and they didn't seem to notice.

CHAPTER 15

THANKFULLY, BY THE TIME SHE returned from trick-or-treating, the séance was long over. No sign of her mother's friends remained, except for the giant, crusty cauldron on the stove.

"How was it, Cee?" Gaby called from her bedroom.

"Fine," Clara replied, pulling off her antennae and dropping her bulging pillowcase on the floor. She headed straight to her bedroom before her mother could ask any more questions.

But she didn't sleep well, plagued by dreams about a ghost in the bathroom who was determined to drown her in the tub. At one point the snakes from Lily's crown began to slither out of the drain and wrap themselves around her ankles. She woke up, sweating and breathless and desperately wishing life could just go back to normal.

"I'm sensing some bad energy," Gaby commented at breakfast. She raised an eyebrow at Clara. "Do you want a Super Soothing Lavender Smoothie? I could add some herbs of the sun to brighten your mood."

"No, thank you," Clara replied, shoveling down her cereal.

Gaby continued to watch her, much to Clara's annoyance.

"What?" she finally snapped.

"What do you need, Cee?" Gaby reached for her hand.

What did she need? Where to even start?

She cleared the cobwebs in her throat, then replied, "I want to talk to Elaine." And she wanted to ask her about this Flavia McGrath person, even if Elaine didn't like to talk about her family. She wanted to hear that Flavia wasn't a witch—just an old lady who . . . who cooked a lot of soup or something.

"Oh." Gaby frowned. "Didn't I tell you? Elaine left yesterday on her cruise."

"Her *what*?" Clara dropped her spoon, splattering milk on the table.

"Cruise. To Barbados." Her mother sipped her soothing smoothie. "She went with a bunch of her friends from the seniors' home."

"A cruise?" Clara said. "On a boat? With *people*?" She couldn't believe it.

Gaby nodded. "I would never have guessed she had it in her. But people change. Anyway, she'll be back in a week or so. You can chat then, okay?"

Clara picked up her spoon and nodded, though it wasn't okay. Especially the part about people changing.

The sky was dark and threatening to storm as she walked to school—an excellent complement to her mood. She trudged through the front doors and joined the kids headed to their lockers, avoiding eye contact so no one would talk to her.

But when her locker came into view, she froze. Olivia was leaning up against it, frowning at her phone while typing intently.

"Oh no," Clara moaned.

"Clara!" Olivia looked up from her phone. "Clara Voyant! Oh, I'm so glad you're here!"

No, no, no! Clara screamed inwardly. But she couldn't run away—Olivia seemed like the type who'd chase her down. "Um, hi," she said.

Olivia looked around. "We need to talk."

"Do we?" Clara tried to slip around her to reach her locker.

"Yes." Olivia stayed planted in front of it. "It's about Preston."

Of course it is, thought Clara.

Olivia grinned. "We're dating!"

"Ew, really?" Clara grimaced. "I mean, that's great," she corrected herself. "Since when?"

"Well, just last night," Olivia admitted. "He texted me to ask me out. Want to see?" She pulled out her phone.

"No, that's fine," said Clara. "Congratulations."

"Thanks. Apparently he just got scared when I told him how I felt. He needed some time to process it. Pisces—you know how they are." Olivia rolled her eyes. "Anyway, this means your horoscope was right!" she went on. "I'm so sorry I mistrusted you. Forgive me?" She put a hand on Clara's arm.

"Sure," said Clara. "But look, Olivia, my horoscope had nothing to do with your . . . relationship."

Olivia waved this away. "I know the next round of fortunes comes out on Friday, but can you tell me mine now? I need to know what to do next. And what Preston is going to do next! Tell me his too, okay?"

Clara took a deep breath so she wouldn't scream. "I can't," she said. "Wesley swore me to secrecy. I . . . I signed a contract," she added. It was only partly a lie; Wesley always swore the Newsies to secrecy about their upcoming issues, though she had yet to make anyone sign a real contract.

"She did?" Olivia's eyes widened. "Oh, that is *such* a Wesley thing to do. Darn her!"

"Yeah." Clara made a dive for her locker. "Too bad, right?"

"Wait, I know!" Olivia moved to block her again. "How about you read my palm?" She thrust her hand at Clara.

"I don't read palms," Clara said, stepping back.

"But look." Olivia held her hand inches from Clara's face. "Check out my life line—it's so short! Does this mean I'm going to die?"

"Olivia!" Clara took another step back. "I don't read palms! I don't even know what a life line is!"

A group of kids passing by ground to a halt. "Clara Voyant!" cried the Scorpio boy from the knitting club. "You read palms too?"

"No!" Clara practically yelled.

"Can you read mine?" asked a girl she'd never seen before.

"Get in line!" Olivia snapped. "I was here first, and I have a life line emergency. Check out the love line too, okay, Clara?"

"Everybody stand down!"

"Mrs. Major!" the Scorpio boy yelped, and all the kids spun to face her, including Clara.

But it was Maeve who stood behind them, fists on her hips. "All of you!" she bellowed. "Back away from the psychic! You think you can just ask for your fortune whenever you feel like it?" She snapped her fingers in the air. "That's not how this works! Clara Voyant writes horoscopes twice a month, and *that's it*!"

"Maeve!" Clara blushed.

"But my life line—"

"I don't care about your life line!" Maeve barked. "Get to class, all of you!"

Reluctantly, all the kids turned and shuffled off, grumbling. Olivia glared at Maeve and then turned to Clara and mouthed, "We'll talk later."

Maeve watched them go, then turned to Clara and grinned. "Pretty good Mrs. Major imitation, hey?"

"Pretty good," Clara agreed, finally opening her locker and tossing her lunch inside. "And embarrassing. And amazing. Thank you."

"Anytime." Maeve took a bow. "Oh hey, speaking of acting, at breakfast this morning—ooh, did you have candy for breakfast? I totally did. Two chocolate bars and some licorice." She bounced up and down. "Anyway, at breakfast this morning, my mom said that if I really want to get serious about acting, she'd look into sending me to Parkside High School."

"Where's that?"

"You know. The school Wesley's going to."

"Oh, wow," Clara said. High school seemed like ages away; she'd never even considered where she'd go.

"You'd have to come too, of course," said Maeve. "They have the best journalism program. Plus, the school's in your old neighborhood."

"Wait, what?" Clara nearly dropped her textbook. "You mean High Park?"

Maeve nodded.

"Really?" Clara paused to imagine it: she and Maeve going to school together in High Park, getting out of Kensington Market and away from the woo *every single day*. "That sounds perfect!"

Maeve nodded. "We could take the subway together. My mom said the school is right next to High Park station."

Clara recalled the high school near the subway station: it was a big, stone building, with stained-glass windows and an unnaturally green lawn. When she was very little, she'd believed it was a castle, until Elaine had informed her that it was just a private school.

"Oh wait," she said. "It's a private school."

"Yeah." Maeve grimaced. "We'd have to wear uniforms. But whatever, it would still be fun. Think about the subway!"

Clara turned back to her locker. It would be fun. It would be wonderful. And it would also be expensive. She didn't know exactly how expensive, but she knew Gaby couldn't afford it. She told Maeve as much.

Maeve frowned. "Well, maybe there are scholarships or something."

"Maybe," Clara mumbled to her locker.

Maeve paused a moment and then said, "You know what? It's years away. I probably won't even get in—it's super competitive."

"Yeah," said Clara. Except she suddenly knew that Maeve *would* get in. She knew it the way she'd known that Maeve would get her part in the school play. It was an odd feeling—a feeling of complete certainty, like a puzzle piece snapping into place.

Was it a clairvoyant feeling? she wondered. Then she shook her head hard. That was all nonsense. All woo.

"Hey, are you okay?" Maeve asked.

"Yes. Sure," Clara said, shutting her locker. Although she wasn't okay. She wasn't even close.

CHAPTER 16

"CLARA!" LINA INTERCEPTED HER
at the door to Mr. B.'s classroom. "I need to talk to you."

"I can't tell personal fortunes, Lina," Clara sighed, exhausted from telling kids that same thing all day. "Writing two rounds of horoscopes a month is all I can handle."

Lina wrinkled her nose. "I don't want my fortune told. I just want to talk."

"Oh." Clara straightened, relieved. "Okay. Hey, what happened to you?" She pointed at Lina's right wrist, which was wrapped in a thick, white bandage.

"Wesley," Lina said darkly.

"Wesley did that?" Clara gaped.

"Mm-hmm." Lina nodded grimly. "By upping the publishing schedule."

"Uh, come again?" said Clara, who'd been picturing the editor-in-chief snapping Lina's wrist with her bare hands.

Lina held up her wrist. "*This* is what happens when I'm forced to produce two comics a month! The doctor thinks it's carpal tunnel syndrome. Do you know what that is?"

Clara nodded; Sophie suffered from carpal tunnel syndrome too, from scooping ice cream for hours on end. She considered telling Lina about the healing poultice her mother had made with arnica and aloe. But she sensed Lina wouldn't want to hear about it.

"Two issues a month is too many," said Lina. "You agree, don't you?"

Clara shrugged. "I guess so." Even one round of horoscopes per month was too much for her.

Lina nodded. "A lot of us feel the same, especially the kids on the production team. Wesley made them work all weekend long! One guy couldn't even go trick-or-treating last night because she dragged him to the print shop to proof the next issue."

"Yikes," said Clara. "So are you going to talk to her about it?"

Lina shook her head. "She won't listen—she's too concerned about her high school portfolio. So." She leaned in closer. "I'm bringing in the big guns."

Clara stepped back. "Meaning . . . ?"

"I'm forming a union!" Lina whipped a piece of paper out of her sketchbook and handed it over.

"A union?" Clara looked down at the paper, which featured a hand-drawn fist holding a rolled-up newspaper. "Newsies Unite!" it proclaimed in big, bold script. It went on to list the working conditions the Newsies deserved, including weekends off and at least three weeks to complete a comic.

"It's an organization that protects workers' rights," Lina explained.

Clara knew what a union was—she'd learned about them in social studies. She wondered whether the time Lina had spent on her flyer might have contributed to her carpal tunnel syndrome, but she decided not to ask. "Thanks." She tucked the flyer away. "I'll read it later, okay?"

"I'll let you know when I organize our first meeting. But keep it quiet for now, okay?"

"Oh, I will," Clara assured her. Wesley would lose her mind if she found out.

As the Newsies filed in for their meeting, Clara could see that Lina was right: everyone looked tired. One of the production kids had his head down on the table—likely the one Wesley had dragged to the print shop the night before.

"Okay, Newsies, we need to talk about the state of the *Gazette*," Wesley began, placing her palms on the table. "I need to see even more investigative pieces in future issues. Our articles are okay, but they're not quite good enough."

Lina set down her pencil. "Not good enough for what, Wesley?" she asked. "Parkside High?"

Sienna and Matt gasped. Clara turned to her in disbelief. Was Lina blind? she wondered. Wesley was wearing a *pitch-black blazer*!

Wesley's mouth fell open. "What did you say?"

"You want an investigation?" Lina barreled on. "Well, here's one—how about you tell us whether you upped the publishing schedule just for the sake of your portfolio!"

All heads turned to Wesley.

She looked like she'd been slapped. "Of course not!" she cried. "I mean, yes, I need a good portfolio to get into Parkside. But more importantly, I care about the success of the *Gazette*! More than anyone," she added, casting a glance around the table.

"I care about the *Gazette*," Lina said. "But I care about its staff too. Which is why I'm starting . . ." She leaned over and unzipped her backpack.

"Oh no, don't do that," Clara whispered.

Lina whipped out a poster. "A union!"

"A union!" the Newsies buzzed.

Clara curled her toes inside her sneakers, wishing she could creep away and hide in another room, like she did when Gaby and Elaine started arguing.

"You can't start a union!" Wesley gasped.

"We want weekends off!" Lina shouted. "And holidays! And three weeks to produce a comic strip!"

"This is middle school!" Wesley wailed. "We don't have unions!"

At this point, Mr. B. wandered into his classroom to find it erupting into chaos. For a moment, he stood in the doorway, clutching his coffee and staring blankly at the unrest. "Um, what's going on?" he asked eventually.

At least Wesley and Lina could agree on that. "Nothing!" they yelled in unison.

Mr. B. blanched—Clara could tell that he, too, wanted to creep off and hide in another room. Then he looked longingly over at his desk, where his calendar proclaimed that he still had 157 days left until retirement.

"Out in the hall," he sighed. "Both of you."

Wesley and Lina glared at each other, but they followed him out into the hall to continue their debate. Once they were gone, the Newsies exploded into chatter. Several started texting their friends with the news. Preston even sneaked up to the door and snapped a few photos of the quarrel in the hallway.

"Lina has guts!" Matt declared.

"Yeah, but Wesley does too," said Lizzie. "And she can't back down if she wants to get into Parkside. Competition is fierce!"

Clara had been trying to forget Maeve's latest news all day, but now it muscled back into her thoughts. She pictured her best friend heading off to high school in High Park, leaving her to fend off the witches and weirdos of Kensington Market all by herself.

What if she was stuck there *forever*?

The thought made her shudder from head to toe. That couldn't happen. She couldn't let it.

"You are in charge of your destiny." That's what Elaine always used to say, especially on days when Gaby was fretting about an ominous horoscope prediction or some planet in retrograde. "You can't decide what will happen to you, but you can decide how you'll react."

You are in charge of your destiny, Clara told herself, and she pulled out her notebook and wrote it down for good measure. That made her feel a bit calmer, but the question remained: what could she do to make sure she wasn't stuck in the Market forever?

Maeve *had* mentioned something about scholarships to Parkside High. Possibly she could get one, if she could prove her chops at the *Gazette*. Could she put together a first-rate portfolio like Wesley's? she wondered. She had almost three years to try—maybe it was worth a shot.

But how could she do that if Wesley wouldn't let her write investigative stories? She chewed on her pen, thinking hard as the Newsies continued to debate whether Lina or Wesley would back down first.

I *could* just write an investigative article and send it to Wesley, she mused. That would be an unsolicited article, which Wesley didn't approve of. But what if the article was *so* good and *so* investigative that Wesley just couldn't say no? It would look as good in her portfolio as it would in Clara's. Everyone would win!

"Yes," Clara whispered, and pumped her fist under the table. Then she jotted down the plan in her notebook. It wasn't foolproof, but it was definitely worth trying.

A few minutes later, Wesley, Lina and Mr. B. all slunk back into the class, and the meeting resumed. No one mentioned the union or Wesley's portfolio for the next half hour, for which Clara was thankful. When the meeting finally ended, she didn't hang around. Maeve had already left, which meant Clara would have to walk home alone. But this time she was glad. She had some serious planning to do.

She was already considering article ideas as she zipped up her backpack and slammed her locker shut. Maybe another cafeteria menu item needed investigating. Like the French fries—could they actually be turnips in disguise?

It was a possibility, but not a great one. She kept thinking.

As she passed the office on her way to the front doors, she caught sight of Buzzter's empty podium and paused to look at it. Could that be her unsolicited article? she wondered. It would be *such* a good story.

Wesley had said that if she wrote it, she'd be breaking the Journalists' Code of Ethics. Clara still didn't understand why. She stared at the podium a minute longer, and then turned and hustled out the door.

*

"I'll be upstairs!" she told her mother as she barged into Healing Herbs. Without waiting for an answer, she ran through the storage room, up the stairs, down the sour-smelling hallway and into their apartment.

A quick online search for the Journalists' Code of Ethics brought her to a list of the principles journalists ought to live by. It was a very long list, including everything from verifying information and identifying sources to never copying other journalists' work.

But there was nothing, as far as Clara could see, about writing a follow-up article to another journalist's story.

After all, she wouldn't be copying Preston—her story would be completely different. It would be, well, a real story.

Had Wesley been wrong? she wondered. *Could* Wesley be wrong?

She opened her backpack, pulled out her notebook and flipped to the notes she'd taken on the disappearance of Buzzter the Honeybee a few weeks back.

"It would be *so* good," she murmured.

The apartment door clicked open and the beaded curtain jangled. "Cee!" Gaby called.

"In here!" Clara yelled back, hoping her mother wouldn't want to chat.

Gaby poked her head into Clara's bedroom. "Want to come help me?"

"Make dinner?" Clara asked. It was the last thing she wanted to do.

Gaby shook her head. "We've got leftover pumpkin soup. I'm about to do something very exciting, and you can help if you want."

Clara waited.

"Paquito came into the shop today. Apparently my philter hasn't helped him sleep—he's still got insomnia. So I'm bringing in the big guns!"

What is it with people and their big guns today? Clara wondered.

"I'm going to concoct my first potion!" her mother declared. "I've got all the instructions in Flavia's grimoire. Want to help? We can use the new cauldron!"

No, Clara thought. *That* was the last thing she wanted to do. Casting a spell with her mother was infinitely worse than making dinner. She recalled Paquito standing in line at Sophie's, unable to choose an ice cream flavor, and she felt pretty certain a potion would not cure whatever ailed him. But she didn't want to debate witchcraft with her mother. "I have a ton of homework," she told her.

"Oh." Gaby looked disappointed. "Well, okay. But let me know if you change your mind. You can help me chant!"

Clara forced a smile. She would not be helping anyone chant, not even for Paquito's sake. She waited for her mother to leave before opening the laptop.

She was going to find Buzzter the Honeybee and write a hard-hitting investigative article about his disappearance. An article that would prove to Wesley Ferris that Clara Costa had chops. An article that would hopefully, eventually, get her out of Kensington Market.

But where to start? she wondered just as her phone buzzed with a message from Maeve.

I'm at the secondhand clothes shop, looking for a detective costume. Come help me?

Clara grimaced. Sifting through piles of stinky old clothes was only slightly more appealing than helping her mother concoct a potion.

Except, she realized, who better to help her brainstorm how to find a kidnapper than someone who'd watched nearly every crime show ever made?

I'm on my way, she told Maeve.

CHAPTER 17

"IF I'VE LEARNED ONE THING FROM watching nearly every crime show ever made," said Maeve, "it's that the criminal is often the least likely suspect." She pulled a dingy leather jacket out of a pile of clothes and slipped it on.

"Least likely suspect," Clara said, noting this in her book. "Got it."

Maeve glanced in the full-length mirror propped up against the wall, and then shrugged and slipped the jacket off. "It's the person you'd never think would do it," she said, continuing her search. "Sometimes it's even someone who's involved in the search for the criminal. Like . . . like Mr. Devlin!"

"Mr. Devlin?" Clara raised an eyebrow. "But he's so upset about Buzzter's disappearance!"

"Exactly," said Maeve. "Maybe it's just an act. An attempt to cover up his crime."

"Maybe." Clara noted it in her book, though she was still skeptical.

"How about this?" Maeve slipped on a blue trilby hat. "Does it scream *Molly Mumford* to you?"

"It screams, 'I'm full of lice,'" said Clara. "You really shouldn't try on secondhand hats."

Maeve snorted. "I think it's a keeper. But I still need a jacket." She kept searching. "Anyway, we have to think about motives too. Who might have had a reason to kidnap Buzzter? And keep in mind that it happened after school, so whoever did it had after-hours access."

"Hmm." Clara chewed on her pen, thinking hard. "Oh! What about Mr. James, the administrative assistant?"

Maeve held up a monocle to her eye. "Tell me more."

"Well, he sits next to Buzzter's podium all day long," said Clara. "Maybe he just got sick of staring at his creepy googly eyes. You can't really blame him."

Maeve gasped.

"What?"

"Look. At. This!" She reached into a pile and pulled out a small tawny-brown blazer. "Doesn't Wesley have one like this?"

Clara reached for the blazer and held it up. Sure enough, the chest pocket was monogrammed with the letters "W.F." "It *is* Wesley's," she said. "Or, it *was* anyway. I guess she has so many blazers that she has to give some away?"

"Wow." Maeve slipped it on. "This is totally Molly Mumford. I'm buying it. And the hat too!" She tucked both under her arm, and they headed for the front counter to pay.

"I should get home," Maeve said as they stepped outside the shop. "I'm starving. And my mom said she'd help me practice my lines after dinner. Opening night is only five weeks away!"

"Oh. Okay." Clara was disappointed that they hadn't cracked the case, but at least they'd made a start. "I'll go home and think about more suspects. Let me know if you come up with any, okay?"

"Will do," said Maeve. "And Clara?"

"Yeah?"

"We've got this. Clara Voyant and Molly Mumford are going to find the Buzz-napper and make them pay!"

"Right," said Clara. "Or maybe just write an article about them."

Maeve shrugged. "Have it your way." She set her new blue trilby on her head and skipped off down Kensington Avenue.

Clara returned home deep in thought. Mr. Devlin and Mr. James were okay suspects, but for some reason, neither felt right. But who else could it be?

"Cee!" her mother cried from the kitchen when Clara stepped through the beaded curtain. "You're right on time. I've just gathered all my ingredients."

"Oh, right. The spell." Clara kicked off her shoes and headed for her bedroom. "I'll be in here if you need me."

"You're missing all the fun!" Gaby called after her. Then she began to read from her grimoire. "Boil water . . . that's done. Light two amethyst-colored candles . . . check. A pinch of deadly nightshade for mild sedation . . ."

Deadly nightshade? Clara shook her head and sank down on her bed. She pulled out her notebook and opened it to her very short list of suspects.

"The least likely suspect . . ." Clara murmured. "Who has access to the school after hours . . ." She tapped her chin, thinking hard. And then it came to her.

"Mrs. Major!"

She couldn't believe she hadn't thought of it before! Supposing Mrs. Major had been dusting the office after school one day and accidentally knocked over the podium with her massive biceps? Clara pictured it: Buzzter tumbling off his podium and smashing open on the floor! Stale Tootsie Rolls scattering every which way! Mrs. Major hastily scooping up his remains and stashing them . . .

Clara frowned. Where would you hide the remains of a giant papier-mâché bee? Would she have just garbaged him? Or was Buzzter . . .

She gasped. "Compostable."

Papier-mâché was just paper, flour and water! Completely biodegradable! If Mrs. Major had anything to do with his disappearance, Buzzter could be in the compost bin behind the school!

Clara sat up straight, recalling how the custodian had barked at her to get away from the bin when she'd tried to peek in. "It smells," she'd declared, but what if it *didn't*? What if it actually contained the gruesome remains of the KMS mascot?

A crash in the kitchen made her jump.

"Oops!" cried Gaby.

"What's wrong?" asked Clara.

"Oh, nothing!" her mother called back. "Just overdid it on the nightshade. Hmm. Well, hopefully he'll sleep even more soundly."

"Mom, don't kill Paquito!" Clara yelled.

"I'm not going to kill him!" her mother huffed. Then she added, "But thank you for your faith in my abilities, Cee. I'm almost ready to chant—come join in?"

"No, thank you!" Clara returned to her work. She had a good feeling about this new theory—a knowing kind of feeling. A puzzle piece snapping into place kind of feeling.

Was it . . . a clairvoyant feeling?

"No." She shook her head and went back to her notes.

But . . . what if it was?

"Oh *no*!" Gaby wailed from the kitchen.

"What?" Clara leaped up off the bed. "What's wrong?"

"I'm missing amethyst crystals!"

"You're missing . . ." Clara sighed and sank back down. "Jeez, Mom. You're killing me."

"I can't do this without the crystals," her mother moaned. "Darn it. It'll have to wait until tomorrow. Poor Paquito has another sleepless night ahead of him."

Clara shook her head, turned back to her notes and underlined Mrs. Major's name. She pictured the custodian slamming the cover of the compost bin just as Clara had been about to peer inside.

She felt it again—that puzzle-snap feeling. Now Clara was certain.

Mrs. Major was hiding something.

CHAPTER 18

"YOU'RE SURE YOU'LL BE OKAY?"

Maeve asked the next day after school.

"I'm sure," Clara said, though she wasn't at all. All day long, she'd been imagining the various ways her compost investigation could end (running away from a furious Mrs. Major, hiding in a locker from a furious Mrs. Major, carried off on a stretcher thanks to a furious Mrs. Major . . .). Now she had a stomachache.

"I wish I could come with you," Maeve pouted.

"Me too," said Clara. "But you can't miss your first rehearsal. Where's your hat?"

Maeve pulled her blue trilby out of her locker and set it on her head. "Look, you have to text me if anything goes wrong. Anything. Got it?"

Clara nodded, not wanting to think about what might go wrong.

"I know! Let's have a code word, in case there's an emergency and you don't have time to type a full message. Hmm . . ." Maeve wrinkled her nose, thinking. "Maybe *cantaloupe*?"

"Cantaloupe?"

"It has to be something weird—something Mrs. Major won't understand if she sees you typing it."

Clara pictured herself cornered by the fierce custodian, quaking in the presence of her giant fists. Would she have the wherewithal to pull out her phone and text Maeve the word *cantaloupe*? How did one even spell *cantaloupe*, anyway?

"I'll be fine," she told Maeve.

Maeve didn't seem convinced but eventually straightened her trilby and waved goodbye, leaving Clara to her mission.

She lingered at her locker for a while, pretending to organize its contents until most everyone had gone home and the hallway was quiet. Then she grabbed her notebook, pocketed her phone and set off for the parking lot.

But when she reached the back door, she found a group of seventh grade kids clustered in front of it. "Shoot," she whispered. She couldn't let them see her investigating the compost bin. Being known as the school clairvoyant was bad enough—she didn't want to be the school dumpster diver too.

She was just about to turn back when she noticed a familiar face in the crowd. It was Olivia, and today she was wearing a one-piece mechanic's suit, paired with silver high heels. Beside her stood Preston Paisley, holding her hand.

Olivia looked her way and flashed a big smile above Preston's head. "Thank you!" she mouthed.

There was no point in going over it all again, so Clara just gave her the thumbs-up. As the group shuffled out the door,

Preston pulled out his camera to snap Olivia's photo. He was still snapping when the door banged shut behind them.

"That's crazy," Clara muttered, shaking her head. She hadn't made anything happen for Olivia and Preston—or if she had, it was entirely by accident. Then she recalled what Lily had said on Halloween night: that Clara's predictions were accurate only when she'd composed them with one particular person in mind.

But that was crazy too. Wasn't it?

"Keep your head in the game," she admonished herself. This was a journalistic mission—it had nothing to do with clairvoyance.

She hurried out to the parking lot, jogged over to the big green bin, made sure no one was watching and pushed open the lid. Then she readied her phone to photograph the evidence, and she peeked inside.

On first glance, it looked like a pretty normal compost: a mixture of apple cores, sandwich crusts, eggshells and grass clippings. But as she studied it, she began to see the rich green and brown tones Mrs. Major had described, like olive and moss, ocher and russet. Clara didn't know much about compost, but even she could see that this was a nice one (though it did smell a bit, like Mrs. Major had said).

What she couldn't see was any sign of Buzzter—no black-and-purple stripes, no googly eyes. Possibly Mrs. Major had buried him at the bottom of the bin, where no pesky reporters would find him. Which meant Clara would have to climb inside and dig around. Which would be absolutely disgusting, not to mention humiliating if someone saw her.

She closed the lid and ran back into the school.

As she hurried back to her locker, she tried to come up with a Plan B—something that didn't involve submerging herself in decomposing food scraps. Could she talk to Mrs. Major again? she wondered. She couldn't very well come out and ask if the custodian had kidnapped Buzzter. At best, she'd simply deny it. At worst, Clara would end up in a neck brace, like the kid who'd tracked dirt on the newly waxed floors.

But maybe I can be subtle about it, Clara thought. Maybe I can pretend to be writing a follow-up article about the green bins, and somehow shift the conversation to Buzzter's disappearance.

She stopped and chewed on her lip. It wasn't a great plan, but it was more appealing than swimming in compost.

She headed for the janitor's office.

Mrs. Major's door was closed, so she knocked quietly. No one answered. She waited a minute and then knocked again, a bit louder.

Still no answer.

She put a hand on the doorknob and turned it, expecting to find it locked. But the door opened.

"Um, Mrs. Major?" she called softly. "Are you in there?" She wasn't.

Clara knew she ought to close the door immediately. She'd seen enough of Maeve's crime shows to know that entering a scary place uninvited never ended well.

But she could also sense a story just beyond the door. She could feel it.

She looked left and right, and then slipped inside the custodian's office.

It was a small space, not much larger than a closet, and packed with mops and brooms and buckets. In the center of the room stood a small table, topped with a few books, a bottle of bleach and several copies of "Mrs. Major's Composting Dos and Don'ts."

And a mysterious object covered in a sheet.

A mysterious object roughly the size of Buzzter the Honeybee.

"Whoa." Clara stepped toward it. Had Mrs. Major been hiding him here all the time? And if so, *why*?

She had to do it. She had to know. She grasped the sheet and pulled it off the object.

It wasn't Buzzter.

Or rather, it wasn't the Buzzter she knew.

"*What are you doing here?*" Mrs. Major bellowed.

Clara shrieked and spun around. The custodian's face was Ripe Tomato red, her nostrils flared like a fire-breathing dragon's. "I . . ." Clara gasped. "I'm sorry . . . I . . ."

"*You're trespassing!*" Mrs. Major thundered.

"I . . . I know," Clara whispered. "I'm sorry. I just . . ." She glanced at the object on the table, and then back at the custodian. "D-did you make this?"

"That's none of your business!" Mrs. Major lunged for the sheet.

"Wait!" Clara reached out to stop her. "Wait, please. This . . . this is incredible."

Mrs. Major looked down at Clara's hand on her forearm, and Clara immediately withdrew it. "No, it isn't. I mean, not yet. It needs work."

"But . . . but it will be," Clara ventured. "And . . . you made it, right?"

Mrs. Major paused, then nodded.

"Wow," said Clara.

The original Buzzter had been lopsided and lumpy. The Buzzter on Mrs. Major's worktable was a real sculpture, masterfully molded out of clay. It actually looked like a hornet, with delicate wings, a sharp stinger and eyes that seemed, somehow, to sparkle.

"It's a work of art," said Clara.

"It's a work in progress," Mrs. Major huffed. "I still have a lot to do, especially on his legs. You have no idea how hard it is to sculpt hornet legs. He'll look better once I've painted and—"

"Mrs. Major, you're an artist!" Clara cried. Mrs. Major shushed her. "Sorry," she whispered. "But you're an artist!"

The custodian shook her head. "I *was* an artist. But that was years ago, when I was much younger." She ran a hand over Buzzter's head and her expression softened, like it had when she'd gazed at the rich tones of her compost bin.

Clara couldn't believe it. Not only was Mrs. Major an actual artist, she was showing signs of real human emotion! She stared up at the custodian, who suddenly didn't seem quite so terrifying. I really don't know her at all, Clara realized. Did anyone at KMS? Emboldened, she asked, "So what happened to the real Buzzter?"

"No one knows," said Mrs. Major.

"Really?"

Mrs. Major nodded. "Let's be honest, it's not a huge loss. Buzzter was ugly."

"Totally," Clara agreed.

"But a school needs a mascot," Mrs. Major went on, "and Mr. Devlin is convinced that Buzzter's disappearance has spelled bad luck for all the sports teams. It's probably just a coincidence but . . ." She shrugged. "Anyway, I knew I could make a new Buzzter—I majored in sculpture in art school. I even won a scholarship to study in Paris for a year." She paused for a moment, staring at a shelf lined with all-purpose cleaners, or possibly something far beyond it. Then she shook her head. "I didn't think it would take this long— I thought I'd have him back on his podium in a week. But I'm out of practice, and these legs . . ." She frowned at Buzzter's limbs, which she'd meticulously etched with tiny hornet hairs.

"Right. Okay." Clara drew a breath. "Mrs. Major, this will make a perfect story for the KMS *Gazette*—"

"No," said Mrs. Major. "Definitely not."

"What? Why not?" Clara cried. "It's perfect!"

"No one wants to read about me," said the custodian.

"Yes, they do," said Clara. "I mean, they'll want to read about *this*. No one knows you're an artist!"

"*Was* an artist." Mrs. Major pulled the sheet back over her sculpture. "I gave that up a long time ago. I'm just doing this to help the school."

"Why did you give up your art?" Clara asked.

The custodian stiffened, and Clara wondered if she'd gone too far. But after a moment, Mrs. Major replied, "Someone once told me I'd never make a living at it—that I should get a real job instead."

Clara summoned all her journalistic courage to ask one more question. "Do you regret it?"

Mrs. Major thought for a moment. "Sometimes," she said. "You shouldn't do what other people want you to do with your life. You should stick with your own dreams."

Clara nodded, thinking of her own situation. Who would have thought Mrs. Major had such wise advice to share? "So is that what you'd tell the KMS kids who want to be artists?"

Mrs. Major considered this, and then nodded. "I mean, as long as they clean up after themselves. Art is messy."

"Okay," said Clara. "So how about we tell them that in my *Gazette* article?"

Mrs. Major hesitated.

"I know they'll be inspired," Clara added. At least, she hoped so. "And we won't publish the article until you're ready to unveil your masterpiece." She wasn't sure how she'd explain that to Wesley, but she'd figure it out later.

Mrs. Major looked at Buzzter again, and Clara saw the tiniest hint of a smile on her lips. Mrs. Major was capable of *smiling*. Would wonders never cease?

"Fine," she said finally. "Let's do it."

"Yes!" Clara almost hugged the custodian, but she stopped herself just in time. Instead, she offered her a hand to shake. Mrs. Major nearly crushed it. Then Clara pulled out her notebook, readied her pen and began taking notes for the investigative article of the year.

CHAPTER 19

ONCE SHE HAD ALL THE NOTES SHE needed, Clara thanked Mrs. Major and dashed out of her office and down the hall.

"No running in the halls!" Mrs. Major bellowed after her.

"Oops! Sorry!" Clara slowed to a brisk walk, headed for the front door. She planned to go straight home, shut herself in her bedroom and write the entire article from start to finish. If it all went smoothly, she might send it off to Wesley that very evening. The headline was already taking shape in her head:

Bee-lieve it or not: Buzzter is back, thanks to a mysterious KMS artist!

As soon as she hit the sidewalk, she broke into a sprint.

"Cee!" her mother sang out when she burst through the door of Healing Herbs. "You're right on time to witness something amazing!"

Once again, Paquito was perched at the counter. He waved at Clara.

"Hi." She stopped to catch her breath. "What's up?"

"I've got amethyst crystals galore!" Gaby held up a plastic bag full of purple gems. "Terence made a quick trip to Mystic Mart for me today. Wasn't that sweet of him? So now I'm going to concoct Paquito's sleeping potion, right here before his very eyes!" She swept her arms over an assortment of ingredients on the counter, including purple candles, several jars of herbs and a box of deadly nightshade. Behind her, the cauldron burbled on the little hot plate Gaby kept in the storeroom.

"Here? Now?" Clara looked from her mother to Paquito. He shrugged, looking a little uncertain.

Although she longed to dash upstairs and start on her article, Clara had a feeling she'd better stick around. It was the feeling she'd had standing outside Mrs. Major's door: that puzzle-snap feeling of certainty. She still didn't know what that feeling meant, but now she knew not to ignore it.

She took off her jacket and set down her backpack.

"So how was school?" Gaby asked as she set two candles up in their candleholders and struck a match to light them.

"It was . . . interesting." Clara leaned against the counter next to the horoscopes Gaby had posted for customers to read while they waited. She couldn't very well tell her mother what had happened with Mrs. Major, at least not with Paquito there.

She ran a finger over the newspaper taped to the counter, recalling how she'd felt—known, actually—that the custodian was hiding something. And she *had* been—just not what Clara had thought it would be.

Did that mean she was a clairvoyant? She didn't know. But something was going on.

"Now for the deadly nightshade!" Gaby dropped a tablespoon into her cauldron, and then threw in two more. "We're going to have you asleep in no time, Paquito!" She checked her grimoire and tossed three amethyst crystals into the cauldron. It bubbled and burped.

Paquito had been looking out the window. "Oh yeah, great," he said, turning back to Gaby and Clara. "I could use that."

The bell on the door jingled, and all three looked up as Sophie walked in. She smiled. "This looks like a party."

"Sophie! You've come for your poultice, haven't you?" said Gaby. "I've got it right here." She rummaged through a drawer and pulled out a small glass jar. "Smear this stuff on your wrist three times a day, or whenever it's bothering you. We'll kick that carpal tunnel syndrome to the curb!"

"I hope so," said Sophie. "The people need their ice cream." She winked at Paquito.

Just then, one of the purple candles tumbled out of its holder onto the counter next to Gaby's grimoire. A split-second later, the grimoire began to smolder.

Clara yelped. "Fire!"

But Paquito was already on it, whipping off his cap and using it to smother the blaze.

"Oh my gosh!" Gaby cried. "I'm sorry, guys! I should have made sure those candles were stable." She picked up her grimoire and inspected its singed pages. "Thanks so much, Paquito."

"No problem," he said, setting his cap back on his head.

"I'll let you get back to your . . ." —Sophie waved at the cauldron— "project." She left some cash on the counter, pocketed her poultice and hurried out.

Clara looked back at Paquito, whose face was still flushed. She could tell he was unsettled, but she wasn't sure whether it was due to the fire or the potion being concocted before his very eyes. He kept glancing at the door, possibly planning a quick escape.

Something's up, she decided, and it's not insomnia. She watched him for a moment longer and then had a crazy thought. "Paquito," she said, "give me your cap."

"My cap?"

Clara nodded, holding out her hand.

"Um, okay." Paquito took it off again and handed it over.

"Why do you want his cap?" Gaby looked up from the ashes she was wiping off the counter.

Clara didn't answer, knowing the explanation would sound completely bonkers. But plans that sounded completely bonkers seemed to be working for her that day, so she tried to recall what Lily had said about holding onto a meaningful belonging while predicting someone's future. She felt the cap in her hands and concentrated on the taco chef, who was looking at her like she'd lost her mind.

And there it was, once again. That puzzle-snap feeling.

"Oh my gosh," she said.

"What's going on?" Gaby demanded.

"Paquito!" Clara turned to him. "You're in love!"

His face turned from red to crimson.

"Wait, *what*?" Gaby threw her hands in the air.

"Right?" Clara pressed on. "You are! With Sophie, the ice cream maker!" She stabbed a finger in the air.

"No!" Gaby gaped.

Paquito opened his mouth, and then shut it. He looked from Clara to Gaby and back to Clara. Then he sighed. "Yeah," he admitted.

Gaby gasped. "That's why you can't sleep! You don't need a sleeping potion, you need a *love potion*!"

"Oh no." His eyes widened, and he shook his head. "I don't think so."

Clara wasn't sure about that either. She turned to Paquito, ready to interrogate him further, but he'd already hopped to his feet. "Maybe I'll come back tomorrow," he said. "I've got salsa to make." And before they could argue, he made a dash for the door.

"You forgot your cap!" Clara called after him, but he was already gone.

"Cee!" Gaby switched off the stove. "This is so exciting! My first love potion! I know there's a recipe in here some-where." She began to leaf through her singed grimoire. "But wait. How did you figure that out?" She looked at the cap in Clara's hands, and then back up at Clara. "Were you . . ." —her eyes grew wide— "using your powers?"

Clara's head was spinning. "I think . . . I'll go upstairs for a while."

"Oh. Yes." Gaby nodded vigorously. "Drink some water.

Maybe even lie down. Do you want me to come with you?"

Clara shook her head. "I'm fine." She headed for the storeroom, then climbed the stairs slowly, trying to sort out everything that just happened.

Halfway up the stairs, her phone buzzed in her pocket.

Well?! How did it go? **Maeve wanted to know.** What did you find?

Clara didn't know how to answer, or even where to start. Over the past two hours, she'd found out that Mrs. Major was an artist, that Paquito was in love with Sophie and that Clara herself . . . well, she just might have psychic powers.

"Whoa." She sat down on the top step in the darkness of the sour-smelling hallway.

What she hadn't found, however, was Buzzter the Honeybee. Which meant there was even *more* to the story. Somewhere out there was a most unlikely suspect who had access to the school after hours and who, as Maeve had suggested, might even be involved in the search for the criminal.

Clara blinked in the darkness.

Someone like . . .

Like . . .

She stood up and ran back down the stairs.

CHAPTER 20

"CLARA VOYANT!" MR. HEALY-LIN SAID when he opened the front door. "How's my favorite—"

"Fine," Clara puffed, breathless from her run through the Market, across College Street and a few blocks north to the Healy-Lin house. "Is Maeve home yet?"

He raised an eyebrow. "This sounds important."

Clara nodded. "It is." She willed him not to ask questions.

"She's upstairs. I'll call her."

But no sooner had he turned around than Maeve came barreling down the stairs, still wearing her detective hat. "Is that Clara?" She leaped down the last five steps and landed like a panther, ready for action. "What's going on? What happened? Did you find Buzzter? Are you okay?"

"No. And yes. And Maeve . . ." She took a breath. "I need the blazer."

"The what?"

"Wesley's blazer. Do you have it?"

Maeve blinked. "No. I mean, my mom brought it to the

dry cleaner this morning. She said they should probably clean it because, you know . . . bedbugs."

"The dry cleaner!" Clara smacked her head. "No!"

"Clara!" Maeve grabbed her shoulders. "What's going on?"

"We need to get it back," said Clara. "Where's the dry cleaner?"

"I have no idea!"

They both turned to Mr. Healy-Lin, who was looking at them like they had just dropped in from another planet.

"Where's the dry cleaner?" they shouted.

"On College!" He pointed southward. "Maybe two blocks west."

"We're going!" Maeve grabbed her coat off the rack.

"Wait," Mr. Healy-Lin said, still looking profoundly confused. "I think they close in a few minutes."

"Then we need to go now!" said Clara.

"Yes!" yelled Maeve.

"Wait!" Mr. Healy-Lin threw his hands up. "*Why?*"

"I have no idea!" cried Maeve. "But Clara does! And we are a team!" She punched the air, then bounded out the door. "We'll be back in, what, half an hour?" She looked at Clara.

"Sure." Clara nodded. They turned and ran down to College Street, and then headed west.

"Up ahead! I see it!" Maeve pointed as she dodged a couple holding hands. They drew up to the dry cleaner just as a man inside flipped a sign on the door from YES, WE'RE OPEN to SORRY, WE'RE CLOSED.

"NO!" Maeve banged on the door, and the man leaped back in alarm. "Please let us in!"

He shook his head and pointed at the sign.

"Please!" Clara called. "It'll just take a minute. We promise!"

He eyed them for a moment and then slowly opened the door. "What do you want?"

"My mom brought a blazer in earlier today," said Maeve. "It's small and brown and we need it back. For . . ." —she looked at Clara— "something."

"Something important," Clara added. "Like . . ." She looked back at Maeve for help.

Maeve snapped her fingers. "A ring!"

"A ring?" Clara and the man said in unison.

Maeve nodded. "I left it in the pocket of my blazer. It's a priceless family heirloom. Belonged to my great-aunt, um, Maude."

"That's right!" Clara said, impressed with Maeve's ability to make up stories on the spot. Clearly acting lessons were life lessons. "We need to get that ring back."

The man looked from Maeve to Clara and frowned. "Let me check. I know which blazer you're talking about, and I don't think we've cleaned it yet." He let them inside the shop, told them to wait and disappeared into the room behind the counter.

"Oh my gosh, this is so fun," Maeve whispered. "Even though I still have no idea what's going on."

Clara nodded, though she didn't think *fun* was exactly the right word.

Minutes later, the man emerged, carrying Wesley's brown blazer.

"Yes!" Maeve and Clara shouted.

Clara stepped up to take it. "I just . . . need a minute," she said. Then she stepped back and held the blazer in both hands, like she had with Paquito's cap. She paused for a moment to remember a time, not long ago, when she had led a normal life that didn't involve predicting the future through articles of clothing. Then she closed her eyes and thought about Wesley Ferris. She pictured her presiding over a *Gazette* meeting, fingertips tapping on her laptop, pearl earrings dangling over her shoulder pads . . .

Puzzle-snap.

She opened her eyes. "Yes," she said. "I thought so."

"Thought what?" Both the man and Maeve were staring at her, wide-eyed.

She handed the blazer back to the man. "You can clean this now."

"Uh, thanks," he said. "But what about the ring?"

Clara looked at Maeve, who bit her lip. "Oh. Um. I . . . just realized that I actually left it at home. Sorry. My bad."

The man blinked at them, then whirled around. "Am I being punked?" he demanded. "Is someone filming this to post on YouTube?"

They backed toward the door, assuring him that wasn't the case.

"Thank you for your time!" Clara called, as they dashed out the door and back down College Street.

"I have NO idea what just happened!" Maeve yelled as they ran. "And now you *have* to explain!"

"Okay." Clara slowed to a walk to catch her breath. "I will. I promise. I'll tell you everything . . . on the way to Wesley's house."

"Wesley Ferris? We're going to *Wesley Ferris's* house?"

Clara swallowed. "Yeah. You know where she lives?"

Maeve nodded and pointed north. "She's three doors down from Maddie. About five blocks that way."

"Great. You lead the way," said Clara. "And I'll explain."

❧

"Incredible," Maeve breathed after Clara had summed it all up. "Mrs. Major, an artist?"

"A good one," Clara confirmed.

"And more importantly, you. A clairvoyant!"

"Well, maybe." Clara still didn't like the sound of that. "I mean, further research is necessary."

"But wow." Maeve shook her head. "I mean, I know I've been calling you a clairvoyant lately, but I didn't really think you could . . . you know . . ." She waved her hands at the sky.

"I know," said Clara. "I can't believe it either."

"It's bonkers. And really cool. And . . . maybe scary for you?"

Clara nodded. "All those things." She was glad Maeve could see all three—and that she didn't seem freaked out by the prospect of her new best friend having psychic powers.

"Can you . . . maybe not tell anyone? Just for now?" Clara asked.

"Of course." Maeve crossed her heart. "I am an excellent secret keeper, you know. Remember Bianca Esposito's pants?"

"I still don't know who that is," said Clara. But she was relieved. She had a lot of thinking to do.

"Here we are." Maeve stopped in front of a three-story brick house, similar to her own but with a red tricycle on the front lawn.

Clara stopped beside her and took a deep breath. She hadn't actually planned what they would do when they reached Wesley's house. But before she could determine the best course of action, Maeve was marching up to the door. She knocked three times, then motioned for Clara to join her.

A minute passed, and no one answered. Maeve knocked again and pressed her ear to the door. "I think I hear someone."

Clara pulled her back. "Maybe we should stop and think—" she began, but a crash inside made them both jump.

"I'll get it!" a child yelled. A moment later, the door swung open to reveal a boy, about eight years old, with blond hair like Wesley's, but long and wild. He smiled at them, seemingly unconcerned by the fact that his T-shirt was soaking wet. "Hi!"

"Hey there," Maeve said casually. "Is Wesley here?"

The boy nodded. "She's upstairs." He held the door open wide.

Clara was about to tell him that he really shouldn't invite strangers into his house, but Maeve poked her in the ribs. "Just go."

They stepped inside the Ferris house.

Whenever Clara had imagined Wesley's house, which she'd done regularly since the first week of school, she'd pictured a scene out of a lifestyle magazine: gleaming white walls, plush carpets, perfectly pressed curtains over squeaky-clean windows. The order of Elaine's duplex combined with the comfort and style of the Healy-Lin home. The kind of place Clara longed to live in.

Wesley's real-life house looked nothing like that. In fact, if Elaine had been there (not that Elaine would have dreamed of showing up on someone's doorstep uninvited), she might have passed out at the sight.

The living room floor was barely visible under a sea of toddler toys. Two big Labrador retrievers wrestled on a carpet completely coated with their hair. One of the dogs' tails was striped blue and purple, thanks to a little girl finger-painting beside them on the carpet. Along the walls, bookshelves bowed under the weight of several hundred books and at least that many knick-knacks. A glimpse into the kitchen revealed dishes piled high in the sink and on the counter, and what looked like the remains of a week's worth of breakfasts on the table.

"Whoa," Clara breathed.

"Just . . . whoa," said Maeve.

"I was cleaning my snake tank," the boy informed them.

"Sorry?" They looked down at him.

He pointed to his sopping T-shirt. "It needed cleaning," he said. "Wesley said it was gross. She's in her room because she hates it when I let the snakes out. But I had to let them out so I could clean the tank." He wrung out the bottom of his T-shirt. Water dripped onto his socks.

"Snakes?" Clara glanced around nervously.

"What kind of snakes?" Maeve wanted to know.

Clara didn't. "We'd better go see Wesley."

The boy pointed to the staircase at the far end of the living room. "Last door on the right," he said. "Come see my snakes after, okay?"

They made no promises, but thanked him and headed up the stairs.

"This is insane," Clara whispered, stepping over a menagerie of stuffed animals. "She can't really live here."

Maeve nodded, avoiding a small mountain of underwear. "It's like this crime show I saw once, where the detectives investigated a house owned by hoarders? And they found this decomposing body in the attic—"

"Maeve, stop!"

At the top of the stairs, they headed for the last door on the right side of the hallway. It was shut tight; a sign on the doorknob read GENIUS AT WORK. KEEP OUT.

"I think this is the place," said Maeve.

Clara nodded and raised her knuckles to knock.

"I got your back, Voyant," Maeve whispered.

"Thanks," Clara said. She knocked three times.

"Jeremy, you better have those creatures locked up!" Wesley yelled from inside.

Clara opened her mouth to explain that it wasn't Jeremy knocking, but a Newbie Newsy and her best friend, who, she realized, was still wearing a detective hat. But Maeve had already pushed the door open. Before Clara could stop her, Maeve stepped inside.

Entering Wesley's bedroom was like entering another dimension, or happening upon an oasis in a desert. Here were the gleaming white walls and perfectly pressed curtains of Clara's imagination. The bed was neatly made and the carpet clean enough to sit on, which was what Wesley was doing—sitting on the floor in her pinstriped blazer, typing on her laptop and snacking on a Tootsie Roll.

Clara's mouth fell open. She'd suspected it, but actually *seeing* it made her head spin.

Wesley looked up from her laptop and gasped. The Tootsie Roll fell to the carpet.

Beside Wesley Ferris sat Buzzter the Honeybee. Or rather, he lay there, belly-up, his googly eyes rolling back in his lumpy head, as if he'd been punched in the gut. Which, Clara realized, he actually had—there was a fist-sized hole in his belly, through which Wesley could access the ten-year-old Tootsie Rolls.

"Buzz-ted," whispered Maeve.

CHAPTER 21

"WHAT ARE YOU DOING HERE?"
Wesley shrieked, sitting up straight. "Who let you in? Who said you could come here?" She looked up at them, and then down at poor belly-up Buzzter.

"I . . . Um . . ." Suddenly, Clara had no idea what to say.

"This isn't what it looks like!" Wesley screamed.

"Oh, really." Maeve tipped her trilby and sauntered farther into the room. "So Buzzter just, like, flew here himself?" She tsked. "Tell that to the judge."

"Who *are* you, anyway?" Wesley screeched. "And why are you in my room? Clara, what's going on?"

"That's the million-dollar question!" Maeve proclaimed.

Wesley looked from Clara to Maeve to Buzzter, and her nostrils flared like Mrs. Major's. She looked like she wanted to pummel them both, and Clara briefly wondered who she'd take out first. But then Wesley's shoulder pads sagged, and she crumpled over her laptop with a moan.

"Mm-hmm." Maeve strolled around the room, picking up objects and setting them back down, looking for more evidence of Wesley's crimes. "Thought you could get away with it, didn't you? But you underestimated the powers of Clara Voyant and Molly Mum—"

"Maeve!" Clara hissed.

Wesley covered her face with her hands.

"Maeve," Clara said. "Can I talk to Wesley?"

"What, by yourself?" Maeve looked up from a book she was inspecting on the bedside table.

Clara nodded. She wasn't sure what she would say to the editor-in-chief, but she knew that if Maeve hung around much longer, Wesley would lose her mind.

Maeve looked down at Wesley, who was sniffling into her hair. "Fine," she said finally. "But yell if you need backup, okay? I'll be investigating the snakes." She sauntered out of the room.

For a minute Clara stood there, unsure what to say, as Wesley pulled at her hair and whimpered.

But finally she looked up and wiped her eyes on her sleeve. "Well? You caught me, Clara," she snapped. "Great work. I stole Buzzter the Honeybee."

"I see that," Clara said. She sat down on the carpet, out of arm's reach in case Wesley decided to pummel her. "So, um, why did you do it?"

Wesley grimaced. She looked down at Buzzter and muttered something unintelligible.

"Sorry?"

"For my portfolio!" Wesley yelled.

Clara jumped. "Right. Okay."

Wesley reached inside Buzzter's gut to grab another Tootsie Roll. "Competition to get into Parkside High is fierce," she sniffed, unwrapping the candy. "I have to prove my ability to write, edit *and* manage a team that produces quality publications. I needed more and better investigative articles. So I . . . I planted one."

Clara nodded—it was what she'd suspected, but she still couldn't quite believe it. "And you gave Preston the assignment because you knew he wouldn't do a great job. Right?"

Wesley shrugged, gnawing on her candy.

"And . . . you were going to write a follow-up article yourself?" Clara ventured.

"What are you, a psychic?" Wesley snapped.

Clara let that one go.

"Yes, I was going to write it myself," said Wesley. "I just hadn't decided what the story would be."

Clara was pretty sure this defied the Journalists' Code of Ethics, and she took a quick look at the wall by Wesley's bed to check. But contrary to Wesley's claim, a copy of the code did not hang above her bed.

"That's what I was doing when you came in and ruined everything!" Wesley glared at her, and Clara moved a little farther away. But instead of pummeling her, Wesley proceeded to burst into tears. "I need a good portfolio!" she wailed. "Don't you get it? I need to get into Parkside so I can become a real newspaper editor and get away from this madhouse! Did you *see* the insanity downstairs?"

Clara swallowed and nodded.

"All I want is order!" Wesley went on. "I want things in their place, making sense. My brother collects hideous creatures and lets them slither all over the house. My grimy little sister doesn't understand the concept of staying within the lines! And my parents—don't even get me started on them. Clara, they're professional junk collectors!"

"They are?" Clara gaped. "Really?"

"Well, they collect and sell antiques." Wesley wiped her eyes on her sleeve, leaving tear blotches between the pinstripes. "They have a shop in Kensington Market. You know, the lime-green house?"

Clara nodded. She passed it every day.

"But it's basically all junk, and they keep a lot of it here at home, which means I have to live in chaos. Clara." She turned toward her, wild-eyed. "Last year they brought home *bedbugs*. Have you ever had to deal with bedbugs?"

Clara gulped and shook her head.

Wesley shuddered. "It was disgusting. You have *no* idea how hard I fight to keep the clutter and the kids and the animals out of my space!"

Clara looked around Wesley's pristine bedroom and then back at the editor-in-chief, who, like Mrs. Major earlier that day, was suddenly starting to make sense to her. As an editor, Wesley could make everything neat and orderly. Real life didn't work that way.

"Turn me in, then, Clara," Wesley cried. "I don't care!"

"Yes, you do," Clara sighed.

"Whatever." Wesley grabbed another Tootsie Roll from

Buzzter's gut. After a moment, she offered one to Clara, who shook her head.

They sat there for a little while, Wesley gnawing on her decade-old candy and Clara wondering what to do next. She considered calling Maeve for backup, but she didn't think that would help. Turning Wesley in for her crime didn't seem like the right thing to do either. She was clearly suffering enough already.

So Clara decided to tell her a story.

"You'll never guess what I found out today," she began. And she proceeded to tell Wesley about the discovery that she was still certain would make for the greatest investigative article of the year.

When Clara got to the part about Mrs. Major's former life as an artist, Wesley stopped chewing and froze, wide-eyed. "That's bonkers," she whispered, when Clara had finished.

Clara nodded. "Okay. So how about this," she said slowly, for she was still thinking it through. "How about we both write this story. Then you can put it in your portfolio and say you also edited it. And I can have my name on it too," she added, leaving out the part about her own portfolio. "And . . . and maybe Preston can take photos, so he'll also get a piece of the action. We could do a big feature—a double-page spread. It could be really great! So great that I bet it'll distract people from Buzzter's disappearance."

Wesley blinked hard, and Clara could tell she was picturing it too.

"You'd . . . share the story with me?" Wesley asked. "Even though . . ." She looked over at poor, belly-up Buzzter.

Clara nodded. She would have preferred to write her own article, but it would be worth it to have her first real story in print.

"And even though I wouldn't let you prove your chops?" Wesley added in a small voice.

"I *can* write more than horoscopes, you know," Clara told her.

"Well, I did give you the waste management story," Wesley pointed out.

Clara gave her a "you've got to be kidding me" look.

"Okay, okay." Wesley turned back to Buzzter and absently stroked his lumpy head. "I know you can write more than horoscopes. I guess that was my problem. I can tell you'll be a great journalist—we editors are very intuitive that way, you know. I just . . . didn't want you to be so great . . . yet."

Clara hadn't expected this. "You mean like . . . you thought I might be better than you?"

Wesley shrugged, tracing Buzzter's googly eye with her finger. Finally, she nodded.

"Huh." Clara sat back against the bed, feeling equal parts vindicated and sad for the older girl.

They sat quietly for a little while longer.

"Well, I won't tell anyone," she said finally. "About Buzzter."

"But what about your friend?" asked Wesley.

"What about me?" Maeve asked, strolling back into

the room. Clara smiled up at her, and Maeve settled her fists on her hips. "Are we all good here?"

"I think so." Clara looked at Wesley, who nodded. "We have a plan for the news story about the new Buzzter. And you and I are going to keep *this* Buzzter secret. Okay, Maeve?"

"I am an excellent secret keeper," Maeve said, crossing her heart. "But we'd better ditch the evidence."

"Ditch him?" Wesley's eyes widened. "Where?"

*

Ten minutes later, they were digging into the compost pile in Wesley's backyard, burying the remains of the Kensington Middle School mascot.

CHAPTER 22

"WESLEY FERRIS." GABY SHOOK HER

head as she swallowed the last bite of her taco. "I would never have guessed that she led a life of crime."

"Me neither." Clara stirred the ice in her glass. Paquito's door swung shut as his only other customers drifted out into the night, leaving her and her mother to shut the place down.

When Clara had returned from Wesley's a few hours earlier, Gaby had taken one look at her face and deemed it an occasion for emergency mid-week tacos. Clara couldn't have agreed more; after all that action, she was starving. So they'd hustled across the street and grabbed their usual table by the window, where Clara recounted the events of the day—every single one.

"You must be exhausted," said Gaby.

Clara nodded. But although it was nearly her bedtime, she knew she wouldn't sleep for hours. She still had so much to think through.

Paquito passed by, carrying a bucket full of avocadoes to the kitchen.

"We'll head out soon!" Gaby called after him, but he just waved over his shoulder, as if to say, "Take your time." He'd avoided eye contact with them all evening, but he did bring them extra guacamole on the house, which Clara took to mean that he didn't entirely hate them for meddling in his life. She'd convinced Gaby not to mention the love potion recipe she'd found while Clara was out investigating crimes.

"It looks like a good one," Gaby had said excitedly. "But it'll require a trip to Mystic Mart, so I can stock up on ylang-ylang and rose-colored candles. Maybe tomorrow after school? I'll see if Terence and Lily are free."

Clara had too much on her mind to worry about that now.

"Cee, I am just so impressed with you and your newfound abilities," Gaby said, pushing her empty plate away. "Maybe we could find you a clairvoyance tutor here in the Market. Wouldn't that be fun?"

Clara pushed her plate away too. "No," she told her mother. "I don't think I want that."

"Oh." Gaby looked disappointed.

"Because . . . even if this clairvoyance thing is real," Clara said slowly, still marveling over the words coming out of her mouth, "I don't want it to take over my life. I want to write for the *Gazette* and hang out with Maeve and do normal middle-school things." She thought back to her conversation with Mrs. Major earlier that day. "I have my own dreams, and they don't involve telling people's fortunes."

"But you're so good at—" her mother began.

"I'll keep writing horoscopes," Clara said firmly. "But only once a month. That's it."

"I thought the *Gazette* came out twice a month now," said her mother.

"It does," said Clara. "But I'm pretty sure we're going to go back to the old publishing schedule." Wesley hadn't said so, but Clara just had a feeling.

"Anyway, the point is, clairvoyance might be a part of my life. *Maybe*. But it can't be everything."

Gaby considered this as she munched on a chip. "That sounds wise," she said eventually. "I guess I've been kind of . . . over-enthusiastic about the whole clairvoyant thing, haven't I?"

"A little," Clara agreed.

Her mother sighed. "Sorry, Cee. I just wanted you to have the freedom to explore something that's always fascinated me. Growing up with Elaine, I wasn't allowed to pursue that passion."

Clara couldn't imagine how anyone could be passionate about clairvoyance, but she nodded.

"I mean, I see where Elaine was coming from," Gaby went on. "She didn't want me to get too caught up in magical thinking, which I have a tendency to do."

"Magical thinking?" said Clara.

"You know, like horoscopes and metaphysics and superstition. According to psychological research, some people turn to these beliefs when they feel uncertain and scared. Magical thinking gives them a sense of control."

Clara raised an eyebrow. Her mother was sounding a lot like Wesley Ferris. "How do you know all that?"

"I read," Gaby sniffed. "Anyway, Elaine didn't want me putting too much stock in magical thinking—or getting to know her aunt Flavia—because she wanted me to know that I could change a situation myself. That I didn't need the universe to change it for me. Remember how she liked to tell us that we're in charge of our own destinies?"

Clara nodded, thinking this through. "Is that why you like horoscopes? Because they make you feel better?"

Gaby sipped her lemonade and nodded. "I think so. It's kind of comforting how they tell you what's going to happen. And even if they don't come true—and *I know*, often they don't—they can make you feel like someone or something else is in charge. You know, like I might mess things up now and then, but the universe has this greater plan." She waved a hand at the ceiling.

"You're worried about messing things up?" Clara asked.

Gaby smiled a little sheepishly. "Sure. Sometimes I worry I'm not giving you the best upbringing, since it's just you and me these days. I worry I'm not being the greatest mom."

Clara hadn't expected this. Apparently there was more to learn about her mother as well. "I think you're a great mom," she said. "And we're doing okay, just you and me."

"Are we?" asked Gaby.

Clara shrugged, looking out the window at the Market shops, most of which had closed for the night. Across the street, Sophie was dimming the lights in her ice cream parlor.

"I mean, I miss Elaine," she said. "I miss High Park. But the Market . . . isn't awful, I guess."

Gaby laughed. "Don't get too excited about it!"

Clara smiled. "I mean, I have things now that I didn't have when we lived with Elaine. Like Maeve. And more freedom. Also, emergency taco nights," she added, pointing to their plates. "We didn't do those with Elaine."

"Nope," said Gaby. "Elaine believed in square meals, cooked at home."

Clara shook her head. "Textbook Virgo."

"Aha!" cried her mother. "So you're a believer now too!"

Clara shrugged. She'd been pondering this for the past few hours. "I don't know. I mean, I guess it's possible that if I can learn clairvoyance . . ." —she paused, once again astonished by her own words— "someone else can learn to chart and read the energies of the planets. Maybe," she added. "*Maybe*."

Gaby smiled. "Maybe." She drank the last of her lemonade and then looked back at Clara. "Can I let you in on a secret?"

"Sure," said Clara.

"I have a dream too. I've been thinking about it a lot lately, especially since you wrote that Gemini horoscope about career success."

"Mom, that was for—"

"Maeve. I know. But it made me think about my own career, and what success might look like for me. I like working at Healing Herbs, but I'd love to open my own shop—someplace comfortable, with soft mood lighting, where people can sit and read books and chat on a rainy day."

"Hmm." Clara tried to picture it.

"And I wouldn't just sell herbs. I'd serve tea, maybe even smoothies infused with healing herbs. And potions for people who really need them."

"That would be popular in the Market," Clara admitted.

"But this is the best part." Gaby held up a finger. "I want to open it someplace else—someplace where people really need a healing potion shop. I'm thinking about the financial district downtown, where Elaine used to work. Remember?"

Clara knew it well. She pictured all the blazer-clad statisticians and stockbrokers, accountants and architects, marching between skyscrapers, clutching briefcases and coffee cups. They seemed like unlikely customers for a potion shop.

She imagined what Elaine would say about it. Likely she'd start lecturing Gaby on the risks involved with starting a new business, complete with statistics on how many fail within their first year.

Or maybe she wouldn't, Clara thought. After all, Elaine was on a cruise ship somewhere in the Caribbean Sea, quite possibly dancing the salsa with complete strangers in her personal space. Life was apparently full of surprises. And people could change. Everything could change. Which was scary. And maybe a little exciting.

"So what do you think?" Gaby asked her. "Good idea or bad?"

Clara thought for a moment longer. "Good," she decided. "I have a good feeling about it." A puzzle-snap kind of feeling, actually.

Her mother's eyes lit up. "That's excellent, Cee! Oh, I'm so glad. We should start—" She broke off, glancing over at the door.

Clara turned to see Paquito stepping outside. "Do we need to leave?"

"I don't think so," Gaby said.

As they watched, the taco chef untied his apron and set it on a bench outside the door. Then he straightened his Jays cap, took a deep breath and marched across the street to the ice cream shop. Inside, Sophie was sweeping the floor. She looked up when Paquito knocked on the door and gave him a big smile.

"Whoa," Clara breathed.

"Whoa," her mother agreed.

"I don't think he needs a love potion," said Clara.

Gaby nodded, grabbing the last tortilla chip. "Maybe we'll just have to find someone else who does."

Clara smiled. "Maybe we will."

CHAPTER 23

"I THINK WE'RE READY," GABY SAID,
surveying the apartment.

Clara looked around as well. They'd set out snacks on the
kitchen table and lined up punch glasses on the counter.
They'd cleaned the entire apartment, top to bottom, and
Gaby had even decorated the windowsills with strings of tiny
twinkling lights.

"I've always wanted to throw a full-moon party," her
mother said. "Have I mentioned that?"

"You have," Clara said. They'd been discussing it since
early November, and it was now the end of the month.

Her mother's original plan for a full-moon party had
involved casting a spell in the back alley, which Clara had swiftly
vetoed. Eventually, they'd settled on a small, indoor gathering with their closest friends. Gaby had agreed not to cast any
spells, and Clara had agreed to serve the punch in the cauldron.

She chewed on her lip as she looked around one last time,
and then cringed as the squirrels began scampering on the
roof. She looked at her mother.

"Don't worry," Gaby said. She darted into her bedroom, emerging a moment later with the laptop and a portable speaker. Within minutes, they had music to drown out the squirrels.

Clara nodded. This was good. "But what if the radiator stops working?" she fretted. She didn't want to have to boot it in front of all their guests.

"We're gathering a bunch of people in a tiny apartment," Gaby said breezily. "We'll have to turn off the heat anyway, maybe even open a window."

"Right, but what if—"

"It's going to be great, Cee. It's our long-overdue house-warming party. Can you believe it's almost December already?" She shook her head, and the clusters of little pink seashells dangling from her ears jingled. Elaine had bought them in a shop in Barbados, along with a seafoam-green scarf for Clara. She'd mailed them to Toronto, along with a note that said:

Barbados was bliss, but I miss you both. I'm planning to come visit in the New Year—maybe once the snow has melted.

"A visit?" Clara had looked at her mother. "Where will she stay?"

Gaby had read the note again. "Here, I guess. If she wants to."

Clara bit her lip and nodded. She and Gaby would have some serious planning to do for the visit, but fortunately, they had all winter to prepare. And in the meantime, she had many other things to think about, including the upcoming performance of *The Seventh Slipper: A Molly Mumford Mystery*, and her *Gazette* article about the brand-new Buzzter, which would be published in the January issue.

"If this goes well, we'll have to plan a winter solstice party!" Gaby said, arranging the twinkling lights on the windowsill.

"One party at a time, okay, Mom?" said Clara.

"Right, but wouldn't it be fun to light a bonfire in the park?"

Before Clara could list all the ways that could go wrong, someone knocked on the door.

"Sweet peas!"

Terence and Lily burst through the beaded curtain with their usual chaos and kombucha. They hugged Gaby and Clara, exclaimed over the decorations, swayed to the music. Clara had to admit they were the ideal party guests. Terence had worn his least-tattered suit jacket for the occasion, and Lily had adorned her curls with peacock feathers.

They were definitely weird, Clara thought. But she let them hug her.

"No sign of the ghost?" Terence asked, glancing toward the bathroom.

"Not since the exorcism," Gaby chirped.

Terence had exorcised their resident ghost the previous weekend. This had involved his hanging out in the mango-colored bathroom for three and a half hours, convincing the ghost to move on. Apparently, it had complied after some negotiations.

Though she'd never seen any evidence of the ghost herself, Clara had to admit it was a nice thing for Terence to do. She was slowly warming up to her mother's weird friends—though not yet to their kombucha. She politely declined when Terence offered her a glass, and instead helped herself to the tropical punch in the cauldron.

"We've been scouring the financial district for a shop for lease," Lily reported. "There's not much available right now, but we'll keep looking. We'll find you an ideal spot for your new business, I promise. Something small and cozy, close to a subway stop. And preferably not haunted," she added, looking at Terence.

"Unless the ghosts are friendly," he said, grabbing a crescent-moon-shaped cookie from a plate on the table.

Clara's phone buzzed.

"The Healy-Lins are here," she told her mother, and her stomach turned a flip. Maeve's parents had never seen the apartment before.

"Well, go let them in," said Gaby.

Clara swallowed. "Okay."

She ran down the hallway, which she and Gaby had painted the previous weekend while Terence was exorcising the bathroom ghost. After much debate, they'd decided on a clean, fresh Coconut Sorbet. Gaby had resisted at first—it was, after all, basically white. But even she had to admit it brightened up the hallway nicely.

Clara zipped down the stairs and through the storeroom,

and then opened the door to find the Healy-Lins standing in the back alley.

"We brought Sammy's doughnuts!" Maeve cried, and her father held up a box emblazoned with a gold *S*. Paquito and Sophie appeared behind them, with buckets of guacamole and double-chocolate ice cream, respectively.

Clara ushered them all in and led them upstairs to the apartment. She pulled the beaded curtain aside so no one would get tangled in it, then she held her breath as they stepped inside.

"Oh, it's lovely!" Mrs. Healy-Lin exclaimed. "We lived in a place just like this, before Maeve was born. Remember?" she asked her husband.

He laughed. "I used to bang my head on the slanted ceilings."

"But I adored them," she said.

"I'll give you the grand tour!" Gaby offered, herding them into the living room. Paquito and Sophie followed, arm in arm.

Maeve grinned at Clara and took a moon-shaped cookie from the table. "Geminis love a good party, you know."

Clara rolled her eyes but grinned back. "Oh, I know."

"So, is she coming?"

Clara shrugged. "I haven't heard. I texted her earlier but—"

The beaded curtain jangled, and Wesley Ferris poked her head inside.

"Wesley!" Clara leaped over and pulled the curtain aside. Wesley stepped in cautiously, sporting a bright-pink blazer.

"The door was unlocked downstairs, so I let myself in," Wesley said. "And I bolted it shut behind me," she added. "I've never been in an apartment above a shop before."

Clara swallowed and forced herself to smile. "Well, welcome," she said, as brightly as she could.

"I brought brownies." Wesley thrust a plate toward her. "They're dairy- and gluten-free, so everyone should be able to enjoy them."

"Thanks," Clara said, softening a little. Wesley was as nervous to be there as Clara was to host her.

"Yes! I love brownies! They pair perfectly with doughnuts." Maeve took them and set them on the kitchen table. "C'mon in, Wesley."

Wesley's eyes widened at the sight of the Ripe Tomato paint, but she didn't comment on it.

"Sweet pea." Lily marched across the kitchen, straight for Wesley. "That blazer is to die for! Where did you get it? And is that a monogram? Classy!" She put an arm around Wesley's shoulders and pulled her over to the table to pour her some kombucha. Wesley looked surprised but not offended, and she even complimented Lily on her peacock feathers. Within minutes, they were chatting easily.

Clara shook her head. People never ceased to surprise her.

Her phone buzzed again.

"I'll get it." Maeve dashed out the door before Clara could reply. A few minutes later, she returned with Olivia, Preston and Mrs. Major. Clara's heart stuttered at the sight of the KMS custodian, who looked even more imposing in the tiny apartment. She slipped off her parka and handed it to Maeve, who nearly toppled under its weight.

"Welcome, guys," Clara said. "Thanks for—"

"Oh my gosh, that wall!" Olivia exclaimed. "Preston, look! It's perfect!" She pulled him over to the kitchen wall; moments later, they were staging a photo shoot in front of it.

Clara grinned and turned back to Mrs. Major, who was still standing by the beaded curtain. She swallowed, hoping it hadn't been a mistake to invite her.

"Here." Mrs. Major held out a box. "I made marzipan."

"Marzipan?" Maeve appeared at Clara's side again, peering over her shoulder.

"They're cookies made from almond paste," Mrs. Major explained. Clara opened the box, and she and Maeve both gasped. Mrs. Major had molded—no, *sculpted*—every marzipan cookie into a different shape.

"Are those astrological symbols?" Clara gaped.

Mrs. Major nodded, looking pleased.

"Incredible!" Maeve took the box. "Come get some punch and a gluten- and dairy-free brownie, Mrs. Major. Make yourself at home." She guided Mrs. Major into the kitchen, and Clara blinked in wonder, watching them go.

As Gaby had predicted, the apartment quickly warmed up, so Clara turned down the heat and went to her bedroom to open a window. When she returned, everyone had gathered in the Electric Purple living room, chatting and eating treats. The sight of them all gave Clara an idea.

"Hey, guys," she called, pulling out her phone. "I want to take a photo."

"Oh, great idea, Cee!" said her mother. "Let's capture the magic!"

"I'll take it," Preston volunteered.

"No, I want you in it," Clara told him. She motioned for them all to cluster together. "Smile," she said, and they beamed.

She snapped the photo and then glanced down at the image on her phone. It was perhaps the strangest gathering of people she had ever seen.

And she had to admit, she liked it.

What would Elaine say if she saw it? she wondered. She wasn't entirely sure. But somehow, it felt right to send her a photo of their new life and the people in it. Their friends.

She hesitated for a moment, then texted the photo to Elaine, along with a note:

We're having a party! I wish you were here, but maybe we'll have another when you visit. Can't wait to see you and show you around. XO

Then she went to join the festivities.

Horoscopes

BY CLARA VOYANT

Aries

March 21 – April 19

End-of-term exams are fast approaching, and now is no time to slack off. Don't even think about faking sick to avoid a test, Aries. A forged note might only cost five dollars from the Counterfeit Kid, but getting caught will land you in detention for life. *So* not worth it.

Taurus

April 20 – May 20

Good news! All the hard work you've put into an important project is about to pay off. Competition is fierce, but not as fierce as your own willpower. Follow that dream, Taurus!

Gemini ♊

May 21 – June 20

Geminis attract friends and admirers from far and wide. But even the most lovable Gemini will encounter critics now and then, and a few are headed your way. Don't listen to the haters, Gemini. You're the right person for the job.

Cancer ♋

June 21 – July 22

There have been a lot of changes in your world lately, and the impending new year promises more to come. But this past year has taught you to weather great uncertainty, with a little help from your friends. Don't worry, Cancer. You've got this.

Leo ♌

July 23 – August 22

You're in the throes of new love, Leo. But while you excel at expressing your feelings and talking honestly, don't forget that listening skills are also important. Try sitting back and letting your loved one talk too.

Virgo ♍

August 23 – September 22

You're living the high life these days, enjoying a vibrant social life. But don't forget to take time to rest and relax by yourself. The end of the year is a good time to recharge, and you'll want to be well-rested for an exciting journey in the New Year!

Libra ♎

September 23 – October 22

The holidays are coming up, and you know what that means: it's time to start thinking about your Secret Santa gift. Put some effort into it this year, Libra. And remember that your first idea isn't always your best.

Scorpio ♏

October 23 – November 21

A wise person once told me that people are in charge of their own destinies. You can't decide what will happen to you, but you can decide how you'll react. I know you love your horoscopes, Scorpio (and so do I!), but every now and then, you've got to head out into the world and make things happen for yourself.

Sagittarius ♐

November 22 – December 21

Buckle up, Sagittarius! One of your many side projects is about to attract a big new audience. Soon there will be more demand for your skills than you can handle. Exciting times lie ahead!

Capricorn ♑

December 22 – January 19

The holiday season can bring out the worst in people, so prepare yourself for what's coming. There's no time like the present to start practicing your patience. Take deep breaths,

Capricorn, and if that doesn't work, a lavender-lousewort tea will do the trick.

Aquarius 🌑

January 20 – February 18

It's almost time to unveil your big project, and you're probably feeling apprehensive. You can be a real perfectionist, which bodes well for your work. But at some point, you just have to let go and show the world what you've created. It's going to be great, Aquarius. I guarantee it.

Pisces 🐟

February 19 – March 20

Pisces are known for their big, ambitious dreams, and you're no exception. But life never turns out exactly as you envision, so don't forget to be flexible with those big aspirations. It never hurts to diversify and pick up a few new skills.

ACKNOWLEDGMENTS

As usual, so many friends and colleagues helped in the making of this novel. Marie Campbell, Tanya Kyi, Stacey Matson, Vikki VanSickle, Louise Delaney and Zoe Grames-Webb read early (sometimes very messy) drafts, offered sage advice and didn't give up on me entirely. Lynne Missen edited expertly, treating the story and characters with such thought and care. Eric Simons came up with simple, magical solutions to plot issues when I needed them. Aryne Sheppard took me to see an alarmingly accurate Toronto psychic "for research purposes." Skye Alexander wrote *The Modern Guide to Witchcraft* and Karen Harrison wrote *The Herbal Alchemist's Handbook*; both provided inspiration and hours of fun. Illustrator Christy Lundy brought Clara to life in the dreamy cover illustration. Sarah Howden whipped the manuscript into shape with excellent copyedits. And the team at Penguin Random House Canada was, as always, a pleasure to work with. Thank you all!